STREET CERTIFIED

Book two of the Murdaland Trilogy

MARTIN STOCKTON

iUniverse, Inc.
Bloomington

Street Certified
Book two of the Murdaland Trilogy

iUniverse books may be ordered through booksellers or by contacting:

iUniverse
1663 Liberty Drive
Bloomington, IN 47403
www.iuniverse.com
1-800-Authors (1-800-288-4677)

ISBN: 978-1-4759-1682-9 (sc)
ISBN: 978-1-4759-1684-3 (hc)
ISBN: 978-1-4759-1683-6 (ebk)

Library of Congress Control Number: 2012907412

Printed in the United States of America

iUniverse rev. date: 05/16/2012

STREET CERTIFIED ANTHEM

Life in the hood's never sweet when you're hungry and have no food to eat or quality shoes on your feet. As you feel the agony of defeat and every smile you meet, you greet. Pride won't allow you to cry in the street. Mama's tired and got moral's so she won't cheat even though daddy's not bringing home food to eat. He hustles day and night trying to find a way until he meets a connect. Daddy's no-longer selling nickels and dimes; he's now movin Kgs, makes Gs. and now we have burgers to go with our cheese. Unfortunately, with hustling comes that awful disease many have died from after catching that hustler's greed. Daddy stole his supplier's product and money now he's six feet deep . . . . R.I.P Daddy; "I pray the Lord your soul to Keep." The price for hustling doesn't come cheap and hustling backwards is like suicide even when you're street certified . . . .

By: Martin L. Stockton

Contents

CHAPTER 1

Big Paper was completely drenched with perspiration as beads of sweat poured from his forehead.

He knew he'd fucked up. His cell phone was ringing every five minutes from his two soldiers Chill and Big Reece waiting for him to hit them with G-packs of ready. It was 8am coke heads and dope fiends was out on the strip off of North Ave. looking for that first blast of coke and hit of dope to start their day. Big Paper had a quick money spot for Chill and Big Reece to trap in. The rock cocaine he hit them with usually sold within a few hours. It was good quality product: fish scale supplied by non-other than peoples associated with Kilo's crew. Kilo had the purest cocaine on the streets. Big Paper had purchased so much cocaine from the crew over the past year he could get G-Packs on consignment. He was always good with moving the product. On a good day he would flip three or four G-Packs and count his stacks; it was nothing to make two or three thousand dollars a day.

That was until he started hitting the pipe! Now he smoked more shit then he sold. Big Paper had been posted up the past 48hours smoking coke in the Hotel 6 in Woodlawn with his side chick named Roxy. A tall pretty brown skin girl about 6'0 with long pretty black hair. She was only eighteen years old but looked more like she was twenty-one. She had the potential to be a model but was growing up much too fast with a lot of negative influences and a false sense of security. Big Paper was twenty-two and was fucking Roxy since she was fifteen. He was her first. And he always made sure she had loot in her pocket. He also purchased her first car. A Red 2006 Honda Accord Lx. Looking at Roxy one would never think she got high; especially high from smoking coke.

"Bye Big Daddy." Roxy said kissing Big Paper on his bearded cheek. He stood about 6' 1 a brown skinned brother who was once 220lbs and slightly overweight. But, was now 180lbs and dropping fast due to his recent preoccupation with smoking cocaine over the past few months. He had her drop him off at his car, a 2007 Black Cadi that sat on 22 inch chrome rims, tinted windows, and all the bells and whistles a Luxury Cadillac could have. Big Paper moved quickly to his car. Roxy pulled off just in time.

Kilo's crew had been looking for Big Paper the past week. He hadn't produced any money or product and it was time to pay the piper. Just as he pressed his remote to open the door a black on black tinted Mercedes SUV pulled up beside him: with Shorty, Squirt, and T.T.; three hustlers who sold cocaine for Kilo. "What's goin on playboy? You a hard nigga to reach" said Shorty, stepping out of the left rear passenger door of the Mercedes ML500. His right hand was tucked under his left forearm concealing a black Glock 9mm. "We drove by the trap but Chill and Big Reece said they ain't seen you and you not answering no calls." Shorty now revealed the Glock 9mm motioning Big Paper towards the Mercedes. Shorty stood about 5'5" and was not to be played with. He was short, but deadly! "You need to take a ride wit us Yo." Big Paper was no fool he knew they were either about to kill him or give him a serious ass whipping for fucking up Kilo's product and money. He had neither money nor product. Just a few hundred dollars of his own stash of cash, but not enough to pay for the coke debt he fucked up. Big Paper was a true street certified hustler from the Eastside that sold drugs ever since he was twelve years old. He had a few bodies of his own and feared no one. "Man fuck you Shorty, I ain't ridin no-where wit yall niggas" At that moment, T.T. the taller member of Kilo's crew got out of the Mercedes SUV. T.T. stood about 6'4" and weighed about 280lbs.

He was the one that slapped the shit outta people who failed to pay their coke debt. Big Paper was ready to go to war. He knew if he got in his Cadi to the Tech-9 under the front seat he would have a chance. "I tell you what Shorty. I'll follow yall niggas so we can talk." Big Paper placed his right hand on the door handle. "This ain't no fuckin game son" Shorty said raising the Glock up to Big Paper's head. He peered around the parking lot discreetly to make sure no one was watching them in case he had to bust off; shit was looking kinda gully. The only people out at the moment were a few merchants and venders entering Security Square Mall to set up shop for today's business. No one noticed the possible homicide about to take place just a few hundred feet away from them.

"Man fuck yall bitch ass niggas." smirked Big Paper as he proceeded to open his car door.

POP . . . POP . . . POP . . . POP . . . rang off the Glock 9mm as Shorty squeezed the trigger sinking four 9mm rounds into Big Paper's skull. Blood poured from his bullet rippled face. Kilo's Crew entered the Mercedes SUV and fled the scene as fast as they had gotten there. Merchants had now taken notice as Big Paper's body fell lifelessly to the ground. His car keys were still gripped firmly in his left hand.

Blood and bone fragments covered his driver's side window as they moved closer to the murder scene.

Several of the them were already on their cell phones taking pictures and posting Facebook and Twitter updates, but no one bothered to dial 911.

Squirt wheeled the SUV down Security Blvd. and onto 695 South enroute to Westport to dump off their guns and lay low at Shorty's girlfriends crib in Cherry Hill for a few hours. Today their supplier Kilo would be coming home and what better gift could they give then to let him know they was still holding shit down on the streets. Even though Big Paper brought in good loot over the years he still showed the ultimate form of disrespect by smoking up product that didn't belong to him. Shorty could've cared less what Big Paper did with the product as long as he had the money when it was time to collect.

For that he had to be made an example of. On the streets you can never show any signs of weakness or you could get played; losing respect and street credibility. Both are crucial to a drug dealer on Kilo's level. "Man turn on the radio in this joint" laughed T.T. "Turn on 92Q and see if anybody won them fucking tickets to that Jay-Z concert tonight at Rams Head" "Shit who gives a fuck who else wins nigga" laughed Shorty. "We already got our tickets to that joint. It's gonna be off the chain" . . . .

CHAPTER 2

Three of Baltimore's top MC's were echoing the sound waves on 92Q's Big Phat Morning Show featuring; Marc, Sonjay, and Porkchop. 92Q Jams, B-mores local radio station served the community with current events and up to date gossip; which often lead to much controversy and all the latest hit songs from popular recording artists local and abroad. Some of the local hip-hop recording artists included The City's own, Club Queen, DJ K-Swift, who was known to rock a party. Other local hip-hop artist included Bossman, Mully Man, D.O.G, Young Low, Vega, and DJ Delaney. These were just a few of the talented hip-hop artists from Baltimore, Md. that ranked with the best. Countless other hip-hop artists: Rappers, DJ's and R&B recording singers were also popular in the Tri-State area, like the beautiful songstress, Paula Campbell. Who was known to set a romantic mood with her angelic voice. November 7, 2007 would be one in the archives. It was Jay-Z day in Murdaland. However; not only was one of hip-hops most successful and influential rappers in town to show Baltimore love. Today also marked the release of Peter Grounds, AKA; Kilo. The infamous Drug King pin who was sentenced to die by lethal injection for multiple counts of murder, drug dealing, and extortion. On this day Kilo would be pardoned the death penalty and acquitted of most of the felony charges except possession of marijuana, and illegal use of a firearm.

Kilo's legal team presented an elite case, making a mockery of the prosecuting Attorney 's who anticipated Kilo receiving the death penalty for his heinous crimes ranging from murder, drug distribution, and extortion to money laundering and tax evasion. Kilo had earned millions of dollars in drug monies and owned much real estate, several vehicles, and businesses many of which, were not in his name. He was clever to make sure his assets were well spread out if in event he ever got popped. He'd learned from Drug Lords that had fallen before him like: Bumpy Johnson, Frank Lucas, and Nikki Barnes to name a few. Kilo also held high regards for the local master mind go-getters of B-more such as: Little

Willie, Little Melvin, and Peanut King. All legendary hustlers. The three things Kilo learned and followed the most was the code of respect, honor, and loyalty. That's one of the reasons he wasn't killed in prison; although an attempt was made on his life it wasn't initiated by any of the Drug Lords he worked for. Kilo was a diligent hustler. Between he and his fallen rival Rockman, Kilo saturated the drug market with connects in Mexico, Colombia, the Middle East, and The Mafia's La' Costra Nostra. Kilo was just that nigga. He had the drug game on lock.

Lieutenants and soldiers of his rival Rockman were also incarcerated and everyone knew Kilo was the mastermind behind the massacre at the Dynasty.

One evening Kilo was returning to his cell before lockdown. Two of Rockmans boys approached him from the front while a third grabbed him from behind holding a shank in his right hand. He was able to stab kilo once in the back, missing his lung by inches. As he attempted to stab him again, Jerome exited his cell and punched the stabber in the face, knocking him to the ground. At that moment Kilo regrouped swinging at the other two inmates in front of him. "Come on you pussy as niggas. You want to kill me. Here I am mother fuckers." "Yo shorty, you should've minded your business. Yelled another one of the attackers. "Now your ass is dead too" "Fuck you!" shouted Jerome. "I'm not scared of you bitch." Kilo smiled as the three inmates began swinging at him and Jerome. "You mother-fuckers are good as dead. I know who the fuck you are" "Fuck you Kilo. You killed Rockman. You Gonna die today nigga" Kilo and Jerome fought side by side.

At the moment, sirens went off. The CO 's closed in breaking up the fight.

"What's goin on here? You boys just got some time in the hole" all five men were separated by the CO's and placed in custody. The whole prison was on lockdown . . . .

From that day on anything Jerome needed he got. And Kilo made good on his word too. Upon his release he asked his lawyers to reopen Jerome's case and represent him. For some reason he knew Jerome was set up just as he said.

Although he was no boy scout, he was a stand-up guy and Kilo knew it. He was good at reading people and most of the time his character analysis was on point.

And if it wasn't for Jerome helping Kilo that day he would probably be dead.

CHAPTER 3

Kilo had recruited numerous people into his criminal empire, and he always made sure he looked out for his soldiers and lieutenants to the utmost. Those who were loyal he made sure that not only them but also their families were taken care of. On several occasions Kilo would flip the bill for funeral services for any of his boys killed from drug deals gone bad or stick up boys on the grind. Kilo was still ruthless although he showed love and generosity to his fallen comrades. And those that crossed him due to greed: Stealing his product, money, or was snitching met a fate all not to uncommon to the drug game. Kilo had no problem having those that crossed him executed without remorse. It was a code of the streets. If Kilo allowed himself to be disrespected he would lose street credibility and be considered weak, falling victim like his long-time rival Rockman whom he'd had the pleasure in helping kill personally during the massacre at the club Dynasty.

Needless to say the three members of Rockman's crew that attempted to kill Kilo were found a week later in the prison courtyard with their throats slit from ear to ear. Kilo was not to be fucked wit, he was too well connected. It was obvious from their throat slashes and the way their tongues hung, this was the work of Colombian assassins who were also incarcerated there. Probably in transit;

Colombian neck ties were their trademark. Kilo sat before the courtroom Judge and jury knowing he was going home today. It was just a matter of formality. His million dollar defense team earned Kilo his freedom. His lawyers already told him no witness was willing to testify against him therefore the prosecuting attorneys case would crumbled like a sand castle on the beach. And the beach was all Kilo could think about at this point. He sat calmly in his Sean Jean custom tailored suit fitting to perfection. Kilo couldn't wait to catch his flight to The Florida Keys with his sexy fiancée Tina, a seductive half Black, half Colombian beautiful woman full of poise and grace, but always kept it gangsta; a true ride or die chick that would kill for her man if she had too. Tina sat in the courtroom looking like a million dollars beside Kilo's right hand man K.G. K.G. had remained loyal to Kilo and stepped up to the number one spot during his incarceration. He was the only one Kilo trusted to keep shit moving and on the strength of Kilo the other drug lords embraced K.G. and allowed him to run Kilo's drug empire. Tina was looking fine as ever with her long black silk like hair draping her shoulders down to the midline of her back. Men looked in admiration but dared not to stare because they knew she was Kilo's girl.

Kilo sat cool, calm, and collected as always chillin with his "Cool Hand Luke" grin formed on his face as he smiled thinking about how fine Tina looked in her sexy black mini skirt displaying her long sexy brown legs with no stockings. All he thought about at this point was how bad he wanted to fuck the hell out of her on the sands of Key West. Tina smiled back at him knowing the look he was giving her and couldn't wait to feel him throbbing deep inside her. She quivered just from thinking about him fucking the shit out of her. At that moment her thong was flooded with wetness from her throbbing vagina. Tina always remained loyal to Kilo during his incarceration and even though she used a dildo to masturbate she never allowed another man to touch her body. As far as she was concerned no other man could ever fuck her as good as Kilo; so why waste her time.

Kilo had a way of hitting her G-spot taking her to sexual heights of extreme pleasure; Nor was any man worthy of her love. Kilo treated Tina like a Goddess.

Kilo no-longer sported the lightly trimmed beard he'd worn in prison; he was now clean shaven. Rap, rap, rap slammed the Judge's mallet as he requested the Jury's verdict. The head Juror stood. "In the case of Peter Grounds Aka. Kilo we the Jury find the defendant; NOT GUILTY!!!!" "There we have it. Peter Grounds The federal court of Maryland drops all charges and here by exonerates you of the death penalty. You are therefore granted release from the federal penitentiary with time severed for remaining charges of illegal possession of a controlled substance.

Mr. Grounds you are free to leave."

CHAPTER 4

Kilo had friends in high places. His loyalty in the face of life in prison and the death penalty did not go unrewarded. Kilo was selling cocaine and heroin for not only some of the most feared and notorious crime bosses in Mexico and Colombia.

But also certain crime families in the Italian mob. Every deal possible was offered from the FEDS to get him to give up his connections, however Kilo never cooperated. He was willing to spend the rest of his life in prison or die by lethal injection before ever breaking the code of loyalty to his crime families.

Upon his release Kilo was gifted 1 million dollars cash, a brand new Maserati, a candy apple red Ferrari 360 Modena and the respect of a Mafia DON.

Kilo and his lawyers exited the courtroom swiftly bombarded by news reporters.

Tina was clung tightly to her man's arm. K.G. went the opposite direction to avoid the media. "I'll get up wit you later man." "Aight man, that's whut's up" replied Kilo to K.G. making his exit. "Ohhh shit! Here we go Kilo" stated Kilo's attorney "these son ah bitches are like vultures" News reporters were pushing each other out of the way trying to get Kilo's first statement. One news reporter in particular was Tuck Williams.

Tuck hated Kilo's guts with a passion and always anticipated the day he'd diss him.

Behold, Tuck was front and center. "Are we on dammit" Tuck asked his camera man. Five, four, three two, one . . . . You're on Tuck. "This is Tuck Williams reporting live for the Baltimore evening news" "So Kilo, how does it feel knowing once again you've gotten away with murder. Did your drug lord friends and expensive lawyers get you exonerated. What's next, are you about to flood the City with more drugs" Kilo felt like spitting in his face, but didn't. At that moment his lawyer whispered to him, giving him a quick update on the son of a bitch hot shot reporter standing before him. "You know that son of a bitch just went bankrupt and is pending foreclosure due to his cocaine and gambling addiction.

"Is that right" smiled Kilo looking at Tuck. "You know, Tucky baby. I heard through the grape vine you like to snort a little fish scale yourself. I got a special hook up for you. Maybe that'll save your ass some money so you can pay your bookie and your mortgage so you can get out of foreclosure and your wife won't leave your broke ass—" "Cut-stop the damn camera!" demanded Tuck.

"Turned it off!!" "Don't you dare compare me to you. You dope dealing bastard.

You're a drug dealer and a murderer ""Yeah" Kilo said sarcastically "and you're a hypocrite cause you're a coke head and a fuck up. Now get the fuck out of my face while you still have one" at that moment Tina hulk spit in Tucks face.

"Ohh damnnnn!!!" everyone stared in disbelief as Tina's spit ran down the side of the reporters left cheek. In an instant rage Tuck raised his hand to strike her. "Motherfucka you hit my girl you may as well kill yourself and that ugly ass wife of yours." Kilo stood motionless staring Tuck down. "Let's get the fuck out of here" demanded Tuck. "Let's go!" Tuck and his camera crew vanished in the crowd in a matter of seconds. Kilo winked his eye at his attorney thanking him for that heads up about Tuck's skeletons. News cameras from other reporters continued to roll as everyone pursued a interview with the infamous Kilo. A black stretch Cadillac limo pulled up on Lombard St. destined to the inner harbor where Kilo still owned a high rise condominium overlooking, The Harbor Place.

Although his name wasn't on the deed, technically he still owned it. Kilo was able to maintain a lot of assets this way. He always had them purchased under someone else's name even thought he was the true owner.

The lawyer opened the back door as Kilo motioned Tina to get in. "You need a ride somewhere?" asked Kilo "No, I'm good Kilo. Got another case in forty-five minutes" "Don't forget about that kid named Jerome. I owe him a favor. Send me the bill for all his legal expenses"

"You got it Kilo. I'll take good care of him" "Cool" Kilo seated himself beside Tina as the lawyer closed the limo door behind him. Although he could be ruthless as a cold blooded killer he was still a gentleman. Over the years Kilo had matured from being a street thug hustling rocks on Jack and 10th street in Brooklyn to running his own illicit cocaine and heroin emporium.

Kilo was a legend in his own time. Many referred to him as, The Black Don Corleone. There were many black gangsters before Kilo like Bumpy Johnson, Frank Lucas, and, Nikki Barnes. In addition to the New York gangsters Baltimore had it's own flamboyant hustlers like Little Melvin, Peanut king, and Little Willie. These movers and shakers set the mold for many hustlers coming up in B-More. Kilo had much respect and admiration for all of the gangsters and hustlers old and new that remained true to the game. Regardless of their demise. Like Freeway Ricky Ross and Rayful Edmonds, another two icons in the drug game. Kilo was a hustler and gangster of a new generation and today he escaped the ultimate fate by being pardoned the death penalty . . . .

CHAPTER 5

The black stretch Cadillac limo proceeded onto Pratt St. enroute to Kilo's Condo at 100 Harborview. It was now 9:45 a.m. The Big Phat Morning Show was coming to a close for the day. The Big Phat Morning Show crew were giving away free tickets to callers for The Jay-Z show that evening. Jay-Z was scheduled to perform hits tonight from his tenth debut album; The American Gangster, at The Rams Head Lounge.

Jay-Z was Kilo's favorite rap artist. He could always relate to his creative street smart Lyrics which always gave a true depiction of the drug game and the life style that came with it. "I want tickets to this show tonight." smiled Kilo listening to a local author now featured on The Big Phat Morning Show promoting his new urban novel.

"I want a copy of that book too. Sounds like it's off the chain." Tina opened her $1,500.00 Gucci pocket book revealing two V.I.P tickets to tonights show. "I know you so well nigga, I knew you'd want to go to this show." "Damn, girl. When did you get these?" smiled Kilo. "The other day when K.G. told me the lawyers had your case on lock and that you was gonna get exonerated." "Oh and here," she said handing him 100 crisp hundred dollar bills folded in half wrapped with a rubber band. "Some spending money" Kilo smiled. He was worth millions but hadn't felt a grip in awhile. Tina placed her hand between Kilo's thighs and slid it up massaging his cock. He was rock hard. "I can't wait to show you how much I missed your ass." Sighed Tina. Her pussy was soaking wet. She was ready to fuck right there in the limo. "Give me dat big dick daddy" she said un zipping his pant's exposing his erection placing it in her mouth.

"OH shit!!" sighed Kilo laying his head back on the headrest. "Damn, suck dat dick baby" Kilo placed his hands down and began caressing her beautiful face. Tina swung her hair around brushing it against his throbbing dick. It had been years since she gave him such pleasure. Kilo came instantly as she placed her round full moist lips back around his erection. "AHHH SHIT GIRL!!" sighed Kilo cumming in her mouth. She swallowed it . . . .

Tina quivered as he slid his hand down between her wet pussy rubbing her erect clitoris.

At that moment Tina sighed loudly as she splashed her love juices soaking her thong.

"Oh shit shawty, dat's whut's good" he smiled. "Damn right nigga and don't you ever forget it, this your pussy" Tina grabbed his dick with both hands kissing it gently"

Kilo slapped her on the ass and smiled. "You damn right baby" the limo driver looked forward pretending not to notice the sexual encounter that had just taken place in the back of his limo. However, the erection in his pants brought him back to other realities. "Damn she's fine!" he thought to himself replaying the sexual encounter in his mind he'd just witnessed. The limo driver Curtis drove into the garage exiting the limo opening the rear door for Kilo and Tina. Curtis was in his late fifties. A medium built brown skin distinguished gentlemen from the West Indies. "Have a good evening Sir and Madam. You are one lucky man sir, your madam is quite beautiful and attentive!"

"Excuse me?" replied Kilo. "Oh, your lady sir. Is very beautiful!" Kilo smiled. He'd heard him the first time, he was just fucking with him. "Thanks pops. You stay cool aight" Kilo reached into his pocket, removed the rubber band and peeled off a hundred dollar bill from the wad of loot he'd just received from Tina. He then handed a crisp Franklin to the driver. The rubber band was a symbolic hustlers trade mark. Kilo placed the rubber band back on his wad of Franklins. "Thank you sir" Kilo nodded, as he and Tina walked towards the elevator.

CHAPTER 6

Kilo's seats were R.S.V.P Other than Jay-Z arriving a little late to the show and Porkchop scuffle with one of the bouncers the concert went pretty well. Porckchop, was a die-hard Jay-Z fan and attempted to move closer to the stage to get a better view, however the bouncer had strict instructions not to let anyone close to the stage during the show without authorization. Porkchop and the bouncer exchanged a few words and before they knew it all hell broke loose. A slight mix up in communication turned into a fiery confrontation and Porkchop wasn't one to be pushed around by anyone. Fortunately no one got hurt. After the show Kilo was honored to met his favorite rap artist receiving a signed copy of his American Gangster cd. Tina was speechless, she never imagine meeting; The Roc Boy, himself that night. Kilo was tempted to attend the after party but declined. He was interested in a after party all his own between him and Tina. Tina was a beautiful caramel complexioned sista of mixed ethnicity. Her father was black and her mother Colombian. Her father like Kilo was a hustler who quickly escalated in the drug game. Tina's father Q was known to be relentless. He was born in Baltimore and raised in LA. during the mid-seventies and abandoned as a child at age nine by his mother who died two weeks later from an overdose of heroin. Q was then raised by, Pete Harvey a local pool shark and pool hall owner who taught him how to be street smart and showed him everything he ever needed to know about shooting pool.

That's how Q got his name. He was a beast on the pool table. He was soon known from coast to coast racking in thousands of dollars. That's how he met a lieutenant from the Colombian Cartel named, Emmanuel Rodriquez. It was at a pool game in Miami Florida. Rodriquez and some of his soldiers were out on the town scouting potential coke heads to expand their cliental. Rodriquez wasn't a pool player but he was a gambler and a cocaine dealer. That night he won over $10,000.00 dollars betting on this stranger he'd eventually become best friends with. Rodriquez was fascinated with Q's mean pool game and liked his hustling tenacity. Q stood about 6'2" A tall lean dark brown skin brother that was a spitting image of Kilo. Except Q was a few inches taller.

To see him anyone would think he was Kilo's father instead of Tina's. That was one reason she was so attracted to him. Kilo like her father was one handsome man that had a way with the ladies and they say. "Women always fall in love with men that reminded them of their fathers." The year was 1984. Q was twenty-four years old. Many pool hustlers, drug dealers, pimps, and gangsters would met in many underground locations to gamble, drink, do drugs, and collaborate on illegal and legal business ventures. Q was no exception. Although he had a mean pool game he also had a jive cocaine habit he entertained. During the wave of the seventies and eighties anyone who was anybody either snorted a little cocaine or heroin on the hustling and club scene. There weren't to many hustlers who didn't do one or the other of that era. It was a part of the social atmosphere . . . .

During the eighties the streets of the U.S. were flooded with cocaine which mostly came from Central and South America. It was a lot of controversy about the drug trade during this time because it was mostly financed by The Federal Government under the Reagan administration that initiated a War On Drugs; however was responsible for most of the drugs that had entered America. The same government would implicate and indict one of Americas highest ranking military combat Marines; Oliver North in his participation of the Iran Contra scandal. A political scandal of cat and mouse that always resorted in smoke screens and mirrors deceiving the American public. "Sometimes a lie is less hazardous than the truth." . . . .

CHAPTER 7

During the mid-eighties Colonel North was implicated in organizing and participating in the transportation of cocaine and marijuana from various locations in Central and South America into the United States, which provided a means to support the Contra rebels.

Lt. Colonel North denied any involvement in drug trafficking however admitted to shredding documents related to the Iran Contra scandal. Regardless of the controversy and denial one thing remained for certain. American streets were being flooded with cocaine and drug dealers from state to state and coast to coast were getting paid, making millions of dollars in pursuit of the American dream . . . .

Freeway Ricky Ross of L.A. and Rayful Edmonds of D.C. were major cocaine hustlers of the eighties known to have made millions of dollars on the city streets of America which inspired such hustlers as Rockman and Kilo. Primary sources of this cocaine came from Manuel Noriega, a former general and military dictator of Panama that worked with the CIA from 1983 to 1989. After countless drug deals Noriega was charged with cocaine trafficking, racketeering, and money laundering in Miami, Florida. He was sentenced to 40 years in Federal prison which was later reduced to 30 years. He is presently being held in a federal prison in Miami and rumored to have suffered a stroke.

Noriega is also facing an additional 10 years in France for money laundering and an additional long-term prison sentence in Panama for murder. Another elite Drug Lord was Pablo Emilio Escobar Gaviria, AKA. El Patron, or El Doctor. This Colombian Drug lord was head of The Medellin Cartel, and listed as the seventh richest man in the world according to Forbes magazine; Pablo Escobar was ruthless as he was flamboyant.

Born with a hustlers ambition, Pablo began his career as a criminal while still in school stealing tombstones and selling them to smugglers from Panama. As a teenager Escobar stole cars from the streets of Medellin and later became involved in other endeavors that catapulted him to a new status. He became known as; The Lord of Cocaine business building an empire during the seventies which would rein in the eighties and nineties.

Making very powerful and wealthy men of drug dealers like Q, Kilo, and Rockman and any other hustler that desired to get money by way of selling cocaine; In pursuit of the American dream . . . .

It is estimated Escobar was responsible for over 4,000 deaths; from Judges to policemen, and many others including snitches that dared to disrupt his criminal empire. Like many other Drug Lords Escobar soon fell victim to his own demise, however it is said he killed himself with a single gunshot to the ear opposed to being gunned downed like numerous family members who were executed by rival Cali Cartels.

The blood-shed, heart ache, and tears from the illicit drug trade was not only isolated to the streets of Colombia. In the United States cocaine was effecting the lives of many people from street users to star athletes like the promising NBA star Len Bias, a natural to the game of Basketball estimated to have been one of the greatest ballers to have ever played the game like Bill Russell, Larry Bird, Magic Johnson, and Michael Jordon. Len Bias was a star athlete out of MD, who died of a cocaine over dose in 1986. The same year he was drafted into the NBA. Len Bias was gifted a brand new Nissan 300zx and was eager to hit the streets of D.C. and MD to celebrate his accomplishments with friends and associates. Some of whom were drug dealers and street hustlers that threw a party for Bias not knowing that day of his over indulgence in cocaine would be his last, shocking the world with his unfortunate and untimely demise.

Len Bias, like many other star athletes and promising youth and adults from Baltimore, New York, D.C. and Va. died a premature, untimely, and gruesome death due to an illicit drug trade sweeping the nation. Regardless of the controversy, drugs and it's affect on America were running rampant at the expense of many promising athletes, actors, and everyday common citizens trying to find their way in an American culture inspired by money, power, sex, crime, and greed. Hustlers Greed . . . .

Q and Rodriquez formed a tight bond that evening. "You know amigo, you are a great pool player" stated Rodriquez sitting across from Q sipping Tequila" "What is your drink?" he asked. Motioning for the sexy barmaid wearing a short black mini skirt displaying her short sexy legs and large breast peering through the V cut of her blouse.

"Mira chica" "Me and my amigo will have another drink" "I'll have a Bacardi and coke" stated Q smiling at the sexy barmaid standing in front of him. She was a beautiful Puerto Rican girl that just moved to Miami with her brother. "I'll have another Tequila" stated Rodriquez in Spanish. "Si-Si" responded the barmaid flashing her beautiful brown eyes. "You like, amigo?" smiled Rodriquez.

"Yeah, she's beautiful" answered Q "Come with me to Colombia amigo, there you will also see many beautiful women. One you may even make your wife"

Little did Rodriquez know his prediction would actually come true.

After a few months of chilling together on the streets of Miami Q agreed to go back with Rodriquez to Colombia. It was 11pm when they left a Miami waterfront Bar.

Rodriquez had just sold his last 4 kilo's of coke to a big time dealer from Dade county.

He and Q had become good friends over the past four months. Although Q still ran game on the pool table his new hustle was selling coke with his mentor and friend from Colombia. Q was a natural hustler. Although he had a cocaine habit himself he never allowed it to interfere with business. That was always rule number one. Only get high on your own supply and never put business second. In the cocaine business Q learned fast that one fuck up could not only cost you your freedom it could also mean losing your life. The first deal he made with Rodriquez was one with a lasting impression. He and Rodriquez met the potential buyers inside a night club on the Miami strip.

Rodriquez always had two extra gunmen with him as back up on all drug deals.

He trusted no one. Q and Rodriquez sat at a table having drinks with two lovely ladies out on the town to alleviate suspicion and the two Senoras were unaware of the fact they were sitting in the presence of High Rollers; selling kilos of cocaine in exchange for thousands of dollars. "Do you want to dance Papi?" asked one of the sexy Latina's smiling at Q. "Go ahead Amigo, enjoy yourself. I'm cool" stated Rodriquez. He knew by the time Q returned to the table his cocaine buyers should be arriving. Q danced to three songs with the sexy Latina working up a nice sweat and a serious hard on that made her pussy dripping wet as they danced the tango.

Q made sure to make periodic eye contact with Rodriquez awaiting his signal to come back over to the table. However, the potential buyers never showed. Two hours had passed, Rodriquez and Q decided to spend the evening with their lustful desires but first they had to get rid of the two kilos of coke. Rodriquez motioned to Manuel and Fillpe who were sitting strapped with Tech-9's under their sports jackets. "Excuse us chica's we'll back in about thirty minutes" stated Rodriquez smiling at the Latinas.

Rodriquez and Q made their exit. However, Q felt something wasn't right. Although he was new to the drug game he was no stranger to the streets. Especially growing up on the mean streets of South Central LA. "Something's not right" stated Q. He noticed two men exchanging words and nodding to two other guys that followed them as they left the table. "What's up Amigo" "I think we've been set up" It's two cats behind us, waiting for us to leave" Rodriquez turned discretely placing his arm on Q's shoulder as if he was attempting to maintain his balance from too much to drink, but in all actuality he was looking over Q' s shoulder to spot their would be assailants.

"Hmmmm" smiled Rodriquez. "Ok amigo, you're right" Rodriquez sat down the leather black bag carrying the two kilos of coke. He then lowered his right hand exposing two fingers to Manuel and Fillpe who remained sitting at their table.

Manuel picked up on the signal and whispered to Fillpe who was sipping his drink.

"It's a setup" he then motioned towards the two men standing anxiously behind Q and Rodriquez. Rodriquez was strapped with a 357. Magnum. Q had a 10 inch switch blade knife on his waist. He wasn't into the gun scene quite yet.

Rodriquez and Q waved to their sexy Latina's exiting the front door with the stick up boys on their trail. Rodriquez and Q walked a few feet apart to distract their assailants.

At that moment one the gunmen rushed Rodriquez and the other Q raising their guns.

The gun wailing assailants were from Cuba and had no intentions of buying the two Kilos of cocaine from Rodriquez. Instead they wanted to murder him in cold blood in front of the 16 bystanders outside the club who quickly ran for cover to avoid being shot.

Rodriquez had already cocked the trigger of his 357 gripping it firmly with his right hand in his jacket pocket with his trigger finger ready to squeeze as he exited the club.

Boom . . . . Boom . . . . Clapped off the magnum as two rounds landed in the Cubans abdomen sending him flying backward about three feet. Rodriquez had fired two rounds directly through his jacket pocket, which sizzled with gun smoke. At that moment Q removed his knife stabbing the other Cuban assailant in the neck who'd squeezed off two rounds missing Q by inches. At that moment the other two Cubans exited the club firing off rounds haphazardly at Q and Rodriquez who quickly ducked for cover. Several rounds of gunfire were exchanged. Q removed the tech-9 from the hand of the Cuban he'd just stabbed in the neck, who was now lying in a puddle of blood.

POP . . . POP . . . POP . . . . CLACK . . . . CLACK . . . . CLACK . . . .
rang off the rival gunmen. Manuel and Fillpe exited the club showering
the other two gun wailing assailant with an array of gunfire. Their bullet
rippled bodies feel to the ground spilling blood all over the streets of
Miami. Several bystanders screamed and ran for cover fearing for their
lives.

Q managed to grab the black leather bag containing the two kilos as he
and the rest of the crew made off into the Miami night heat. From that
point on Rodriquez knew Q was a stand-up guy. Not only did he talk
the talk of a true hustler, he also displayed the courage and heart of one;
HE WALKED THE WALK. African-Americans from the US had a bad
reputation and were stereo typed as being untrustworthy, unreliable, and
unpredictable. But from personal experience Rodriquez knew this wasn't
true. Rodriquez had never met a man as honorable and courageous as Q.
From that night on Rodriquez knew Q was someone he could rely on.
That's when he allowed him into the world of his Colombian affiliates.
He knew his boss would be pleased. Rodriquez was a man of loyalty and
respect. His code was death before dishonor. He and his sister Maria were
orphans, their mother and father killed in a deadly gun battle on the street
of Medellin Colombia by rival Cartels. Rodriquez and his sister were
taken in by a local family. Rodriquez grew up embracing the very Cartel
that took the life of his parents.

He was determined to someday be in power. After his next deal of four
kilos Rodriquez and his crew boarded his $150,000.00 Bay Liner speed
boat at The port of Miami destined to Colombia. It was a trip Rodriquez
had made several times. However this time he had his American friend
with him and little did Q know not only would he meet a lustful desire; he
would also met the love of his life that would bare his child; her name would
be Tina. His beautiful princess that would later become the love interest of
Kilo. One of the most notorious drug dealers to ever enter the drug game
exceeding the level many before him and few that followed . . . .

CHAPTER 8

When Kilo and Tina arrived at the BWI/ Marshall Airport. He had no idea they would be traveling to his villa in Key West via a private jet belonging to a Drug Lord of Mexico; of course the 1 Million dollar jet plane would be on a corporate account, lost in the paper trail of crooked corporate executives. It was a trick of the trade; One hand washes the other. Money was power, regardless of how it was obtained;

Someone always had a price. And money was always good . . . .

Kilo and Trina were escorted to the private jet by K.G. "Ok my nigga, you and your lady are on your own from here. I'll get up wit you when you get back from the Keys.

I got some shit to take care of back in LA, glad you out the joint, shit's been crazy"

"Yo that's whut's up" smiled. Kilo. "I got you kid. And for real, I m proud of how you held shit down man. I could always depend on you" said Kilo looking K.G. directly in eyes. "You know how we get down my nigga, "One" "One!" K.G. replied

K.G. Kilo and K.G. exchanged hand shakes and hugged each other with the mutual respect of two military combat generals. "Take care of this lovely lady of yours too" said K.G. leaning over with his 6'7' 210lb. frame kissing Tina on the left cheek.

Kilo and Tina boarded the private jet prepared for take off to Kilo's Catholic Ln.

1100 sq ft villa he purchased for 1.1 million dollars back in 2004 when he was on top of his drug game before being incarcerated. Kilo purchased the property in Tina's name. As with many of his real estate ventures Kilo always made sure to place properties in names of people he could trust. From legitimate business partners to his lovely and loyal fiancée. Commercial flight passengers and airport staff thought Kilo was a celebrity or professional athlete of some sort considering his athletic stature. Needless to say he was a young black male that had it going on. Everyone could tell he was a brotha that wasn't hurting for cash. But little did they know he was one of the most accomplished drug dealers of his time. And regardless of his media attention during his bit; he always liked to remain Lo-key and out of the public eye. But when in a corner Kilo could be a ruthless son of a bitch; without remorse. Kilo had come along way from selling nickel bags of weed and rock-cocaine on the hard streets of Baltimore, Md. and New York City. He was now a made-man selling pounds of cocaine and heroin deep in a drug game that only death could part at his level. The private jet was immaculate, with its plush leather seats and expensive imported rugs. A state of the art $50,000.00 art entertainment system with 50 inch HG T.V., Bose surround system, and the capability of telephone tele-conference via T.V. were also provided. Meaning if Kilo wanted too he could see the person he was talking too on the phone via the 50 inch HG TV set anywhere in the world . . . .

The bathroom had a Jacuzzi bath with 14 KT. Gold knobs and imported marble that displayed an impeccable mirror like shine. Kilo and Trina were flying like the Rich and famous. Crystal glasses sparkled awaiting to be filled with the new Ciroc Vodka, created by none other than one of hip-hops greatest moguls Sean John, AKA Diddy, AKA Puffy Combs. Kilo had heard much about the new Vodka and was ready to indulge. A crystal ashtray contained two chocolate Dutch filled with green. When Kilo smoked weed; if it wasn't a fresh batch of green it was purp. He knew Tina was the culprit behind the marijuana filled Dutch's. because the only time he really liked to smoke was with her and the only time she smoked weed was with him. Kilo and Tina toasted with a glass of Ciroc and got blazed. The sweet stench of marijuana smoke filled the air. Cling, cling echoed the crystal glasses of Ciroc. "Here's to whatever we go through." smiled Kilo. "Always Papi" smiled Tina lying her beautiful face on his broad shoulder.

Damn Kilo thought to himself; she is one fine chick. For the first time Kilo entertained the thought of starting a family. Tina stood behind him through thick and thin. A woman of true loyalty. A true ride or die chick. The kind every true hustler longed to be down with him. Kilo took another puff and passed the weed to Tina who was already in the zone. "I'm good baby." she replied." Kilo puffed again putting the blunt out in the crystal astray. He laid his head back on the headrest. "Damn this some good ass weed" he said, as he glanced out the plane window thousands of feet above ground. How different the world looked from thousands of feet above ground . . . .

"I've never known you to desire nothing but the best baby" Tina always knew what to say to validate Kilo's ego. Kilo took another sip of Ciroc and resumed resting his head.

He closed his eyes and began to reflect on the pass few years of his life. The lives he'd taken and the number of times he almost lost his. Kilo was at a point in his life where he began to entertain the idea of being a father; to have a son to carry on his legacy. If he died today or tomorrow he would have nothing to leave behind but his legacy in the drug game and no seed to carry on his name; however Kilo knew he would always be married to the streets. (Til death did them part!) the drug game would always be his first family and first obligation. He knew too much and was too far up the hierarchy to ever walk away. His only way out the drug game would be death. And even if he got married, the drug game would always be his first wife. Unlike Tina's father Q, Kilo was supplied by multiple Drug lords and it wasn't many drug dealers that could orchestrate that much weight. Kilo was a business genius. He was responsible for tons of drugs entering the United States from Colombia, Mexico, and the Middle East. The drug emporium Kilo managed was phenomenal. He had a lot of people on his pay role and played a major role in stimulating the economy. With drug money came purchasing power. A lucrative business of supply and demand. It's a wonder the government didn't stake an interest in legalizing drugs like it did alcohol during the prohibition during the rise and fall of Al Capone; one of the most honored and respected gangsters to ever live. The taxation of illicit drug sales would generate trillions of dollars.

The Bay liner moved the through the water like a Bass on the hook of a fly rod fisherman. It's nose in the air toppling waves at 150mph. Rodriquez, Q, Manuel, and Fillpe had snorted several lines of pure fish scale cocaine and drank a fifth of Tequila. The bay liner wasn't the only thing flying. They left the port of Miami via The North Atlantic Ocean passing through Cuba, Haiti, and Jamaica through the Caribbean Sea onto Medellin Colombia. And it was still party time. That's when Q met Rodriquez sister Maria. Who would know several years later they would give birth to a beautiful bi racial Colombian Princess . . . .

CHAPTER 9

As soon as the Bay liner hit the pier of the water front club everyone paid homage as if the Pope himself had just arrived. This was Rodriquez's and Maria's club. Rodriquez was smart; although he worked as a lieutenant in the Colombian Cartel selling millions of dollars of cocaine a month. He still used his monetary profits to invest in his future. He sold drugs, but also had a natural business sense which eventually became the rise to his fall. Rodriquez loved and respected The Medellin Cartel, however he was still his own man. So he thought . . . .

Rodriquez grew up poor on the streets of Medellin Colombia, just as Pablo Escobar, Rodriquez was diligent in making his mark in the drug game and soon met the same fate. After the death of Pablo Escobar, members of his cartel soon met the same demise at the hands of their rivals. A valuable lesson that always stayed with Q. After the death of Rodriquez he married Maria and brought her back to the United States. It was then the beautiful Tina was born. Q learned a valuable lesson from Rodriquez's demise. From that point on he made sure to keep nothing but the best bodyguards around him regardless of the price. That's why he pursued the incredible skills of a trained martial artist named Derrick.

CHAPTER 10

Flick, flick, flick snapped Q's business card gripped firmly in Derrick's hand. Derrick continued flicking the card with his thumb as he sat in the living room of his moms public housing in Cherry Hill Homes. A look of triumph crossed his face as he stared at the hundred plus trophies, plaques, and ribbons he won after competing against high ranking martial arts fighters in karate tournaments nationwide. Derrick's mom transformed her living room into a display showcase of martial arts achievement. The accumulation of her son's acceleration and achievement in the arts was evident in the arrangement.

Sixty of the hundred trophies stood 6' tall with (First Place Fighter.) and his name engraved neatly in the center of the brass label. These trophies had been presented to Derrick from high ranking martial arts experts and officials nationwide. From Riley Hawkins to Chuck Norris, and Michael Stetson. These high ranked martial artists honored Derrick for his display of superior martial arts abilities. He was twenty-six years old and his demeanor consisted of an earnest self-discipline and loyal dedication to the art of fighting; As well as, the utmost respect for his instructor named, Sensei-T, who had been severely gunned down three weeks prior to one of Derricks biggest bouts with martial arts kickboxing champion Donald Goodman. Sensei-T had been critically wounded from gunshots fired by armed stick up artists robbing people at ATM's. These malevolent armed thugs where sweeping the East coast in a brutal rampage of tawdry armed robberies taking the life of anyone who dared to intervene their ruthless endeavors.

Sensei-T's intervention of that evenings stick-up capper was truly unprecedented for what he had initially planned for that night. Enroute to the banks drop box to make his weekly deposit of martial arts fees, Sensei-T with his keen observation observed a robbery in progress. The unexpected victim was a thirty-six year old white plumber named, Dennis Chapman. Chapman frequented the ATM particularly on Friday nights.

This was prior to his Charm City rendezvous at Fells point with the fellows in search of sexy hotties whom they might get lucky with; often they would compete for the same girl to see which one of them had the strongest game. Thus far Dennis held the lowest record.

His charm and wit had only landed him in bed with a half-dozen females in the last three months. Aaron on the other hand averaged about one a week. Therefore he was considered the Mack of the four man crew, whose motto was; "The safest sex is protected sex, no matter how fine she was!!" Dennis worked hard during the week and partied hard on the weekends. He and his crew would often pop E-pills before hitting the Baltimore club scene throughout the Fells point area. Dennis approached the ATM booth with card in hand; inadvertently a chilling numbness filled his body resulting from the cold steel tip of a snub nose 357. magnum revolver pressed firmly against the base of his skull. "You yell, you die motherfucka!" a stern tone commanded standing on an angle to the side of Dennis to avoid being seen by the captive lens of the security camera. The armed thug proceeded to instruct his victim, who was now pissing his pants.

"Empty your account or I'm a empty this gun in your head bitch as mothafuka . . . . NOW!" this time the gunman's tone was more stern and demanding. Dennis neuro-impulses were stagnated with fight or flight. He heard the gunmen's demand, but was unable to move. And fighting at this point was not an option. "I'm giving you two seconds motherfuka. Empty your account or I'm a blow your damn brains all over that machine.

I want to see a balance statement too." Dennis's breaths became shallow as sweat poured from his face in the hot summer June night air. His nerved twitched right had shook uncontrollably inserting the ATM card into the machines automatic teller slot.

"Good, now punch in the code and empty dat bitch" the gunmen laughed silently as he notice piss running down the side of his scared victims shoe. "Yo white boy, if I get piss on my shoes I'm a kill your ass anyway!" Dennis fear turned to hate. He was embarrassed to have pissed himself and felt helpless. Not only was he being robbed, he was also being humiliated. An angered Dennis continued to follow instructions knowing his life was about to be over if he attempted to disarm the gunman. Little did he know this was a scare tactic his robbers used on all of their victims. They used intimidation to make their victims afraid for their lives while almost emptying their accounts. The limit of most withdraw' s was six hundred dollars a day. If a victim had more than a $10,000.00 balance they would find themselves being held hostage by their armed robbers making withdraws until their accounts were empty. However this was seldom the case, most of the time these particular stick up artist were content with anything over $300.00 Dennis was one of at least fifty victims they would rob during the course of a day. On an average they would make at least $1,500.00 to $ 2,000.00 a day in the tri-state areas. Dennis reluctantly handed the armed gunman his hard earned cash that would soon be gone in a matter of seconds. At that moment Sensei-T arrived on the scene parking his Black Jeep Cherokee parallel to the banks drop box. He exited his jeep en-route to the drop box when he observed the robbery taking place 10 feet away from him. With the grace of a panther he motioned to close the distance targeting the armed assailant not noticing the other two gunmen standing as lookouts.

Sensei-T made his way over to the crime scene with intentions of distracting the armed gunman. "Oh I see you're giving this gentleman here assistance with his transaction?"

Sensei-T's sarcastic tone and confident mannerism made the gunman feel very uneasy.

The gunman was used to being the one in control making his victims feel helpless and afraid. Sensei-T was neither; nor did he display the least concern he was vis-à-vis a cold blooded killer. "I assume the transaction's a withdraw?" the Sensei's confidence, sense of humor, and resilient smile unnerved the gunman making him feel as if he were the victim. Yet and still he was holding the gun. Staring the gunman in the eyes, he lunged his 6'2" 190lbs muscular frame towards him with the quickness of panther mesmerizing its prey, his breaths were controlled as he channeled his "Ki" this was a form of power derived internally exhibited by martial artist who channeled their energy from three inches below the navel, with a breathing pattern that generated power. "Let him go" commanded Sensei-T in a mild mannered tone of voice. "Let him go and take my money instead" at that moment the gunman's partners of crime closed in from behind standing four feet away. "You should have minded your business, now we gonna take both yall loot" smiled the other gunman holding a 38 special revolver. Sensei-T turned his head slightly in the direction of the gunmen standing behind him without turning completely around. His keen audible sense permitted him a precise location of the gunmen, all he needed to do was make sure they were within striking range. The gunman at the teller machine felt more confident now that his partners of crime had his back.

"Yeah nigga, ain't nobody scared of you, you should've minded your own fucking business" Sensei-T closed in for the kill. Once again he lunged towards the 5'10" slender built gunman locking the his arm snapping it at the elbow like a twig. The gunman screamed an agonizing yell as the 357. Magnum fell from the hand of his broken arm which now swung painfully limp just hanging by tendons, muscle, and flesh.

The bone in his arm was completely broken. He then grabbed him spinning him around absorbing the shots of two bullets fired from the other gunman. "OH shit!" he yelled as he realized he'd just shot his partner in crime. The gunman then fired three more shots determined to hit the Sensei. Sensei-T tried desperately to allude being hit but was shot in the shoulder. As he motioned to turn another bullet hit him in the back. Sensei-T fell helplessly to the ground. Dennis Chapman managed to escape unharmed in the mist of all the gunfire. The gunmen grabbed the bag of money Sensei-T dropped and fled helping his wounded partner in crime as he clung his broken arm tightly to his gunshot body. Sensei-T survived the gunshots, however he would have to spend the rest of his life as a paraplegic. He was only forty-eight years old, but looked to be twenty years younger.

Now he would be confined to a wheelchair the rest of his life. The bullet severed a nerve, causing paralysis from the waist down. Sensei-T would never walk again.

CHAPTER 11

Just 16 years prior to the Sensei's debilitating gunshot wound Derrick's mom enrolled him in Sensei-T's Karate classes at The Cherry Hill community center at the age of ten.

Unfortunately Derrick's dad was never a role model figure. Instead he became a statistic joining the countless number of black men in his era who had fallen by the wayside ; consumed by a never ending cycle of drugs and crime, which inevitably led to his death at the early age of thirty-four. He was gunned down in a drug deal gone bad. Derrick was a small framed ten year old boy with no muscular tone and awkward mannerisms which made him easy prey for neighborhood bullies who would take his school lunch and chase him home after school. On one occasion he and his mom sat in the principals office in attempt to identify his attackers. Derrick was too ashamed to identify them. He knew the result would be in him being teased by his classmates. Derrick could deal with being beat up and chased home, but snitching would really make him feel like a coward. One evening on her way from the supermarket Derrick's mom observed a flyer tacked to a telephone poll, which encouraged parents to enroll their kids in Karate classes; guaranteed to instill confidence and discipline in urban youth. She paused momentarily sitting her heavy grocery bag and a gallon of milk on the pavement beside her. She reached into her old black leather pocketbook draped over her shoulder removing a black ball point pin.

Next, she reached down tearing off a small section of the brown paper bag containing, chicken legs, wings and thighs. Three cans of baked beans, four cans of tuna fish, five cans of Sardines, five cans of mixed vegetables, and a loaf of bread which sat neatly on top. She stroked the ball point pin several times against a section of the brown paper bag pressed firmly against her pocketbook in attempt to start the ink flow. Derricks mom jotted down the Karate instructors name and number. The following Saturday morning Derrick's mom accompanied her son to his first karate class. After the next three sessions she developed a strong apprehension concerning Derrick continuing the classes.

Sensei-T stood an intimidating 6'2" He was a handsome and charismatic brown skinned man with a muscular frame which projected an essence of power. His commands of martial arts instruction echoed the recreation center. An over lapping black belt fitted snuggly around the waist of his karate Gee swinging rhythmically as he paced the recreation floor. At the end of the session Sensei-T approached her. He detected the expression of fear and concern on her face and assured her Derrick was ok.

He stressed to her the concepts and philosophical aspects of Martial arts and that his method of instruction was primarily to instill confidence and discipline in his students, teaching them to over come their fears and channel their anger. With Sensei-T's explanation of his method of instruction Derricks mom felt more at ease.

The following sessions Derrick attended on his own. His mom felt her presence there would distract Derrick and prevent him from reaping the full benefit of being independent; hindering the concept of him building confidence and self-esteem. Derrick excelled in the arts moving up quickly through the ranks. Within five years he was a first degree black belt and earned much respect from his peers. No one dared to bully him anymore. Shortly after enrolling in the martial arts classes Derrick was approached by some of his bullying classmates. Derrick fore warned them that if they proceeded to push him around they would regret it. As one of the three bullies motioned to push him Derrick grabbed his arm flipping him over his back. He then kicked the other bully in the stomach and yelled, "Ki ayyyy" at the third bully who took off running. All of his classmates laughed as the bullies got a thorough ass whipping from Derrick who was no longer gonna take their shit. From that day on Derrick had no other problems from bullies. They all sought to be his friend, or avoided him altogether.

Chapter 12

During the course of the next few years Derrick's mom developed a bad heart condition derived from heredity which was compounded by the pangs of heart disease. At this point in her life. The only hope would be a heart transplant.

Derricks reminiscence of his recent past transformed into a recollection of memories of his moms struggle to get a heart donor, which brought him to a disappointing present.

Just two hours ago he'd performed to the peek of his martial arts ability in attempt to win a championship bout that would earn him $50,000.00 which would be contributed to his moms heart surgery and a opportunity to fight the World kickboxing champion in his weight division. However, due to political corruption and selfish pride he was relentlessly denied his rightful winnings. Derrick was in the best physical and mental shape of his life. His sensory awareness was extraordinary. He trained earnestly for the bout, even though his Sensei had been critically gunned down just two weeks prior to that evenings event. Derrick went on with the match as scheduled as he knew his Sensei would have wanted him too. His competitor was Donald Goodman. A twenty-one year old college dropout who began his martial arts training at the young age of eight. Donald also displayed devastating martial arts abilities, however he was no match for Derrick. Yet and still Donald still had a competitive edge. His father was a corrupt Senator with strong connections. His political power and influence weighed heavy, even in the arena.

The senator was proud of his sons martial arts abilities. Even though he frowned at his academic failure he saw his excelling in karate as a means of compensating for it. Besides it wouldn't look good for his political campaign being that his son was a academic derelict. His winning the fight would demonstrate he was good for something. The senators morals and values of right and wrong; truth and honesty were momentarily ignored. His primary concern was his son winning the fight and his self-centered demeanor would cost him a total of $15,000.00 $5,000.00 to be paid to the referee to ensure Derrick not beating the living shit out of his son. Two of the three judges would also receive $5,000.00 each to rule in Donald's favor. The fight was fixed. Derrick and Donald stood eye to eye in the center of the ring with the poor excuse of a referee standing between them. He announced the preamble of rules and regulations expected of each fighter, which would be a total contradiction to his bogus interventions during the fight. Derrick and Donald both returned to their respectful corners of the ring.

The ear piercing ring of the bell echoed the arena as the tips of the fighters gloves collided and the intense crowd of spectators cheered and applauded. Derrick and Donald closed distance like they were being driven by a magnifying force. Donald proceeded with a series of jabs, which Derrick deflected, countering with a side step and a right hook lading on the bottom of Donald s chin. He then followed up with a left hook kick, snapping it into the back of Donald's head sending him falling into the ropes. Derrick was closing in for a quick finish when the referee intervened stopping the fight with an unlawful ruling, which distracted him allowing Donald to regain his composure. The crowd of angry spectators hissed and booed. The referee's distraction made Derrick susceptible to a series of kicks and punches delivered by Donald knocking Derrick to the canvas. Derrick stood for a standing eight count, which ended with the ringing of the bell concluding the end of the first of the 12 round, 3 minute bouts. Derrick locked eyes with the referee with a look of disgust. The cheating ref was unable to maintain eye contact. Instead, his shameful guilt transformed to a bogus rage ordering Derrick back to his corner. Derrick returned to his corner but refused to sit, he was too pumped with anger and adrenaline. His trainer extended a white towel wiping the blood from Derricks nose and mouth. He then advised Derrick not to lose his composure, but channel his anger resourcefully, using his anger to his advantage. It was obvious to everyone watching the fight that the referee was siding with Donald. The ring of the bell indicated the start of round two. Donald moved towards the center of the ring with a smirk on his face and a false sense of confidence which sent a spine tingling chill of fury through Derrick, from head to toe. Donald landed two jabs to

Derricks jaw followed by a right hook. Derrick ducked the hook landing a lower body punch smashing into Donald's ribs. The impact of the body punch driven by the swivel of Derricks hips and the fury that possessed him lifted Donald off his feet. Derrick followed up with a left upper-cut knocking Donald s body erect. He then jumped to the air with a left snap reverse kick to Donald's forehead which sent him flying into the ropes. Donald's body bounced lifelessly off the ropes and onto the canvas. The referee's facial expression was one of awe, as he turned to view the Senator seated amongst the cheering spectators. If looks could kill the referee would be dead. The Senators bloodshot eyes and angered expression indicated he was not pleased with his observations. Immediately the fearful referee intervened turning his back to Donald who laid dazed and almost unconscious on the canvas and began shouting bogus unlawful rulings to Derrick. Once again the referee was stalling for time trying to allow Donald to regain his bearing and Derrick knew it. Thoughts of a right crescent kick to the ref's head was very desirable at this point. "No Derrick, No don't do it, you'll be disqualified!" shouted his trainer from his corner. Which prompted Derrick's mind back to reason. His primary objective was to win the fight. The referee could stall no longer. He motioned toward Donald with hesitance performing a standing eight count, which was more like a standing sixteen. The combination of cheers, boo's, and hisses echoed the arena. Donald finally stood to his feet and a look of relief came over the ref's face. The fight resumed . . . .

Donald lunged with a jab, which Derrick deflected landing a double instep kick to Donald's lower abdominal region and face. Derrick closed in this time for total annihilation of his opponent; at that moment the referee intervened again proclaiming Derrick executed a low blow. Derrick ignored the referee's bogus call pursuing his opponent relentlessly. The furious referee attempted to push Derrick back, but Derrick was too quick. He side stepped the anxious referee sending him flying head first on the canvas. Derrick closed in on Donald with a flurry of punches and kicks knocking him once more to the canvas. Spectators in the crowed Arena were now standing on their feet.

The referee lost all composure jumping to his feet waving his arms demanding the ringing of the bell and the disqualification of Derrick for un-sportsman like conduct.

The decision of the two judges on the Senators payroll concurred with the referee's ruling. Derrick was disqualified, thus making Donald Goodman the winner by technicality. The horrifying boos of spectators changed to gratifying cheers as Derrick lunged with a jumping side kick to the referee's chest, which sent him bellowing between the ropes and out of the ring. Derrick exited the ring greeted by cheers and pats on the back. "That was your fight man, you no you won that shit!" yelled one spectator.

"This some bullshit, that referee is a fucking fake!!!" stated another angry spectator.

The referee walked over to Donald raising his arm in the air proclaiming him the winner of that nights bout. The Arena grew silent as everyone watched Donald jump around the ring as if he had truly one the fight fair and square. At that moment the crowd of angry spectators began booing denouncing Donald as the victor. Even his corner men appeared to be embarrassed by his accolades. The Senator smiled as he and his entourage exited the Arena intoxicated from his power and persuasion. It was evident, by his demeanor he was not one to lose, regardless of the price. It was true "Absolute power can corrupt absolutely" or was it a character flaw deeply imbedded in the Senator that was exposed by the power he possessed. His actions revealed there was no shame to his game and he was willing to win regardless of what was right or wrong. It was this type of relentless corruption that made a bad name for honest politicians. Q and his entourage were also present at the bout, he had a lot of money waging on the fight.

And even though he knew Derrick was the better fighter, an inside tip was given to him to put his money on Donald which earned him a quick $35K.

Alone in the locker room Derrick changed into a Adidas sweat suit throwing his fighting gear into a black duffle bag. He was too disgusted to shower.

CHAPTER 13

"What the fuck have I done?" he said to himself "I lost control. I fucked up. I allowed my anger to cost me the fight." Derrick exited the Arena by the rear door. By the time he got to the street a white stretch tinted limo was pulling up beside him. The driver quickly exited the limo opening the back door. Seated in the rear seat was Q. donning a white Nino Cerruti suit. During Q's era in the eighties and early nineties Italian designers dominated the fashion industry, providing top quality merchandise at a price that only those with money could afford. Who would have guessed twenty years later with the evolution of hip-hop, young black rap moguls would be playing an intricate part in the fashion industry, such as; Daymond John the founder of FUBU, Russell Simmons with the introduction of Phat Pharm, Sean Combs with Sean John, and Jay-Z and Damon Dash with the induction of Roca wear; The latter group of hip-hop moguls were the dominating trend setters in the new millennium fashions during Kilo's Reign.

Q's affiliation with Rodriquez of the Cali Cartel in Colombia catapulted him to an elite position of power in the drug game. After Rodriquez brutal murder in Colombia Q became a made-man and affiliated with a Drug Lord in Jamaica.

On the way back from Colombia, months before Rodriquez's fatal death. Rodriquez introduced Q to his affiliates in Kingston Jamaica. After three days of partying and meeting money getters like himself Q was pretty much a made man in terms of his organized crime conglomerates. Nothing would stop him from rising to the top of the drug game that only few survived, now Q wanted a top notch drug runner and bodyguard who could handle himself under pressure and Derrick was the ultimate fighter whom he thought would be the man for the job. Q was a definite fan of Derrick and marveled at his martial arts abilities. He had attended several of his matches over the years and always wanted to recruit him into his criminal organization. He had learned from many great hustlers and gangsters before him that, "The whole is the sum of its parts." Only the strong and wise survived the drug game and you would only be successful as the people in your organization, any weak links would cause the chain to break and the penalty; life in prison or death. He had seen too many organizations fall when confronted with adversity. A weak link would snitch under pressure telling all he knew to save his own ass. This was something Q learned not to tolerate, if he even thought someone in his organization was a snitch they would be assassinated by one of his personal hit men.

No questions asked . . . .

CHAPTER 14

Q was now thirty-eight years old. A dark complexioned brother with a neatly trimmed beard that stood about 6'2" currently weighing 165 pounds. A solid, lean, clean cut appearing brother that you would never suspect of being a drug lord. Many players on the West Coast often confused him with Freeway Ricky Ross who was the most paid drug dealer in California during the mid-eighties and nineties. Q was smooth and easy going. Nothing about him appeared ruthless; yet he would kill you in a heartbeat when tested. Q was ruthless as they came. Although he lived a lavish lifestyle he looked ten years younger than his thirty-eight years of life and was a true gentleman. Anyone who didn't know his notorious reputation as a relentless gangster would think Q was a mild mannered businessman that wouldn't hurt a fly. A friendly smile greeted Derrick inviting him in for a chat. It was 8:00pm A glare of light produced by a utility poll outside the Arena on Baltimore St. reflected a blinding light from his VS1 diamond cut, 14kt gold pinky ring that complimented his $80,000.00 14kt gold Oyster dial Rolex watch that also sparkled with hundreds of flawless diamonds. No doubt about it Q was a man with money, power, and prestige. It was obvious by his demeanor. "Excuse me, but are you sure it's me you wanna talk too?" stated Derrick with a tone of uncertainty. As he looked around to make sure Q was really addressing him.

"Yeah young blood, I think you're an excellent fighter. You can make a lot of mulla, dinero. A lot of fucking money working for me! Get in let's talk about it" Q displayed a wide confident grin feeling the triumph and power of his own demeanor, which intensified Derricks mind state of inquisition from the flamboyant gangster sitting before him in the white stretch limo. At this point Derrick felt he had nothing to lose, but little did he know he was about to make a decision that would not only change and affect his life, but it would also impact the lives of everyone he held dear to him.

Derrick tossed his duffel bag on the limo seat opposite Q and seated himself, closing the door as the limo driver proceed to drive per Q's instruction through the open privacy glass. "Drive down the block." Q instructed his driver. "Pull up on the side of the Hustlers Club." The block was Baltimore's late night entertainment district located on Baltimore street. This was where the late night action was and where you could see some of Baltimore's hottest exotic female dancers. A place Q often visited to unwind.

You would think a man of his power and prestige would be nervous about being in the streets, but Q came from the streets and held much respect there and although he was out on the town wearing over a hundred thousand dollars in jewelry, no one dared to rob him, even without the presence of his personal bodyguards. Q was one of B-more's prominent hustlers even though he spent a lot of time out of town he was always welcome home and respected. Q and Derrick exited the limo outside the Hustlers club entering through the side entrance, Q had private booths on every club on the block, there were rumors he was even connected to the Italian Mafia.

Q was greeted by a long time friend Fred who worked as a bouncer at the club. Fred and Derrick exchanged accolades undetected by Q. After a few words with Fred, Q joined Derrick in his private both where he would be entertained by his favorite dancer named, Nikki, a beautiful redbone who stood about 5'5" and a body that was out of this world.

36-24-36. She was only 20 years old, but told everyone she was twenty-0ne. She was a dime. Her long black shoulder length hair would swing rhythmically with her exotic body moves when she danced driving the men crazy, and some of the women too; that liked girls. Q laughed to himself as he looked over at Derrick. He could tell he was green to the night life. He stuck out like a geek with his nervous boy like charm and the ladies loved it. They could tell he was vulnerable prey, but none dared to test him being he was with Q. And little did they know behind his boyish charm was a trained martial artist capable of killing a man with his bare hands. Fred recognized Derrick right away being he was a 1st degree black belt himself. He had fought in a few karate tournaments with him over the years. "What you drinking fighter?" asked Q "O J" answered Derrick, without the least hesitation. Derrick was not a drinker, but did smoke a little weed now and then. He had no shame to his game. The hostess looked a little bewildered, but dared not laugh or mock him. "OJ it is" she smiled seductively. "And I know you'll have the usual" she said smiling at Q. which was Remy Martin on the rocks. All of the hostesses knew what Q liked. He was a regular when he came downtown to the block." I think you're an excellent fighter Derrick and a man of integrity. I want you to fight for me. But not in the ring. I'll explain it to you later.

And don't be discouraged by your fight this evening. It was fixed. That asshole Senator paid off the referee and half of the judges to assure you didn't when the fight so his bitch ass son could win; fucking loser. Everyone knows you won that fight man" at that moment Q handed Derrick an envelope containing two grand. "That's for you young-blood. No strings attached. You deserve it" Derrick was speechless, he'd never held more than a few hundred dollars at once needless to say two thousand dollars in small denominations. The envelope contained mostly tens and twenty's and about two hundred dollars in ones and fives. Q made sure Derrick had a few dollars to tip the girls.

"Relax and enjoy yourself young-blood, and don't spend it all in one place. These girls know how to work a nigga's pockets man" Q was a master at interpreting a persons expressions and character. After all character interpretation was a survival skill he was forced to perfect many years ago in order to maintain a competitive edge in the drug game, which attributed to his ability to see through fake characters that sought to infiltrate his elaborate criminal empire. Q could tell by Derrick's expression he was confused. "Derrick, I know you're probably asking yourself how does this nigga know so much. Dat's because the Senators on my payroll. And that son of a bitch would have paid any price for his loser ass son to win that match" at that moment the hostess returned to the booth with their drinks. This one was on Q as he tipped her with a twenty bill. "Keep the change baby" she smiled kissing him on the check. Q was a master at flattering the girls and they loved him; He would've been a hell of a pimp. He raised his glass for a toast. "So you in young-blood?" he motioned towards Derrick. Derrick lifted his glass of OJ and toasted.

With all due respect Mr. Q I need time to think about this. Q sipped his Remy peering over the rim of his glass. "I'm familiar with your financial dilemma and I know you need money for your mom's heart operation. I have heavy connections Derrick"

Q leaned back with complete assurance as Nikki slid down between his crouch rubbing his erection with her nice soft round ass that hugged her tiny black thong. He had the complete confidence of a master chess player about to check mate. "If you work for me Derrick I'll front you the loot you need for your mother's heart operation, it's your choice?" damn Derrick thought to himself. "How the fuck do he know all this shit?"

Q was on point about him needing fifty grand for his mothers heart operation and this was an opportunity of a life time. At that moment Nikki's long black hair brushed against Derricks temples as she raised up placing her perfectly round 36DD's in his face. Derrick was a man of discipline and self-control however his hormones were in over drive. Nikki smiled as she brushed her hand over his erection and leaned against his thighs. She was a seductress and a natural born aphrodisiac that could make the most celibate man wanna fuck. But this time the seductress was getting hot. Derrick was hung like a horse and she wanted him. Immediately she turned around rubbing her ass against his dick. "Umm . . . . Big daddy" she sighed experiencing a slight wetness in her thong as she continued to ride him. Q smiled feeling the spirit of his Remy as he looked on. You in trouble now young-blood. I think Nikki' s bout to blow your mind.

Nikki was beautiful and deadly. Her pussy was like platinum and she knew it.

It was something about her that could drive a nigga crazy, she'd emptied many a bank account and stash from hustler's trying to play her, but ended up getting played.

Whipped by what only a select few got to experience; her seductive poison. Q hit the pussy twice but was smart enough not to fall in love with it. The only thing he was addicted to was making money. He had even snorted coke on occasion during his run with the Colombians but nothing over powered his hustling game. Q was a hustlers, hustler and if it didn't make money, it didn't make sense. "Have fun young-blood and be careful, she's deadly" he smiled. He handed Derrick his card. Call me when you've decided if you want to work for me" Q exited the club to his private limo, on the way out he told Fred to watch Derrick's back to make sure no one brought him a move.

Derrick was a new face on the block and many a nigga would kill to get wit Nikki and it looked liked Derrick was about to hit that ass tonight. Nikki was stuck to Derrick like glue. It was something about him that was alluring and she wanted him tonight. It was 1:00am and she was ready to go. She would normally dance until 2am She told Fred to tell the club owner she was gone for the night, however a few drunk and coked up customers weren't happy when they saw her leaving. Two nickel and dime hustlers who where posted up at the bar when they say her and Derrick making and exit. "Yo, hell no, where you goin shawty!!" Lil-Mike said grabbing her by the arm. "Get tha fuck off me nigga!" Nikki yelled attempting to pull away from him. "Bitch you ain't finished dancing we tipped your ass a lot of money. You better get your ass back on stage.

Shit! If you leave wit somebody it's wit me!" before Fred could make it across the bar to intervene Derrick removed Mikes hand from Nikki's arm twisting it at the wrist.

"Mother fucker you done lost your mind.!" yelled Lil-Mikes homie Moot as he pulled a 10 inch blade swinging it at Derricks throat. Derrick stepped back and then lunged forward punching Moot in the face breaking his jaw instantly, blood spurted out of his mouth as two teeth feel to the floor. He then grabbed his arm with the knife snapping it at the elbow like a twig. Fred stopped in his tracks staring in disbelief. He knew Derrick was fast but never saw him in action in this type of environment and under these circumstances; Derrick proved to be a true warrior and a nigga not to be fucked wit.

The next ten seconds, seemed liked ten minutes to Nikki; time seemed to come to a complete stop. At this point all she wanted was to get the fuck out of there. She knew Lil-Mike was a good paying customer, but tonight she wasn't feeling patronizing nor in the mood for creating an illusion of lustful desire to a nigga she could care less about, boosting his ego with the flattery bullshit. However what she was feeling between her and Derrick was unexplainable. Something she had never felt before and she was beginning to feel vulnerable. Nikki was always on top of her game, a lot of hustlers and ballers tried desperately to win her heart, but were rejected. Only to find themselves spending lots of money on gifts trying to impress her; she even had a couple of Corporate Executives willing to leave their wives to win her love. There was something mesmerizing about Nikki, especially when she danced; beyond her beautiful body, that looked like it was sculptured with true perfection; her face was also beautiful and full of innocence, especially her beautiful hazel brown eyes that were stunning. She looked a lot like R&B's hit sensation Beyonce; yes she definitely had it going on . . . .

Derrick regained his composure grabbing Nikki by the arm, "Let's get the fuck outta here before I kill one of these sucka ass niggas" she was more than happy to oblige.

"Fred we out, I'll talk too you tomorrow" said Nikki. "You good, go. I'll take care of this mess" . . . . answered Fred scratching his temple, wondering if he should give these two Niggas another ass whipping or just cut-em loose. After all they were good paying patrons; he decided the latter and cut them loose.

CHAPTER 15

Nikki and Derrick arrived at her condo via taxi cab on St. Paul St.. around 1:45am.

"Let's take a shower" she said, grabbing Derrick by the hand walking him to the bedroom. Derrick was speechless. He hadn't been with a woman in two years. Instead, his sexual gratification was derived from a few knuckle shuffles and the latest hottie in the Jet Magazine that resulted in him exploding his semen into the porcelain throne.

Derricks last love interest was his high school sweetheart that cheated on him giving him a VD classified as, gonorrhea. Being consciously aware of Aids and it's effects on careless sex practices, Derrick swore not to go out like that, besides he heard about the hustler named Tyrone that killed a young trick named Lady-T over that shit. After getting burned, Derrick was careful not to ever let that ever happen again. Needless to say he would never go out like the legendary hood star Tyrone.

Nikki walked into her bathroom, which was nothing extravagant, yet possessed a taste of elegance. It was spotless. The bathroom floor seemed to sparkle and the tile walls reflected their appearance. Nikki began removing her clothes and spontaneously Derrick did the same. "I'll be back Boo," she said kissing him on the cheek. Nikki turned on the water of her whirlpool bath walking naked into the living room, Derricks dick stood erect as he watched her perfectly round, yellow ass walk provocatively across the bathroom floor. "Damn, Derrick said to himself! Nikki returned with a Philly blunt, rolled wit sum mean green . . . . It was about to get LOUD!!!!!!

Nikki, turned on her Bose system, which set the mood with some old school Marvin Gaye. Then she lit four candles and turned off the bathroom lights escorting Derrick over to the whirlpool bath tub. She lit the blunt taking a puff handing it to Derrick, without hesitation he took a puff of the blunt and choked a little. Derrick hadn't smoked weed in years since his early teens hanging out with some high school friends in the Cherry Hill projects. Even though he was a kick ass martial artist, he was no stranger to smoking a little weed now and then. Nikki laughed at Derrick's demeanor, she could tell he was feeling the effects of the weed. He even laughed for a moment at himself.

"Ha. Ha I know this song" he said grooving to the music. "That's Come live with me angel by Marvin Gaye, right? off the, I want you album." "Yup" smiled Nikki.

"What you know bout that girl?" smiled Derrick. Nikki took another puff of the blunt and placed it in an ash tray on the side of the tub.

"Set back and I'll show you big daddy" Nikki leaned forward kissing Derrick gently on the lips. He never closed his eyes and neither did she. A small kiss on the lips turned into a passionate steamy exchange of lustful desire as their tongues collided.

At that moment their eyes closed and their bodies connected like two cells becoming one.

Sweat dripped from their bodies as steam of the whirlpool tub bubbled and their tongues rolled in the heat of passion. "Fuck me." Sighed Nikki grasping his erection. "Oh shit."

Derrick thought to himself. I don't have no protection. SHITTT! "Derrick stopped, pushing Nikki back gently. "We can't do this right now baby. I don't have a rubber." Nikki Smiled opening her hand which concealed a Magnum condom. "I know silly, we don't know each other that well yet." Nikki opened the condom wrapper and held Derricks big fat dick in her hand and began donning the magnum condom. Derricks erection throbbed as she unrolled the condom on his dick. She slowly began kissing him again as she lifted up in the tub sliding down slowly on his stiff penis as it entered her wet throbbing vagina. Derrick felt like he was about to explode. He hadn't had no pussy for a while and was a bit too excited and Nikki could tell. She bit him gently on the lip and shifted her position, bending his dick back to make him take his mind off of cumming. Nikki had serious pussy control and knew how to fuck. Derrick's eyes rolled back in his head as he thought he was about to cum but didn't. "Oh shit he thought to him self. Ummmm. Damn. Derrick pulled her forward and began to thrust himself deep inside her. Nikki yelled when he hit her G spot." Fuck me Derrick, yes fuck me good baby!"

Derrick and Nikki fucked for what seemed like an eternity reaching several rhythmical climaxes. "Oh . . . Oh shit!!!" she sighed collapsing in his arms as they both panted with their hearts beating 120 times a minute. Nikki and Derrick gasped for a breath as they continued to kiss and embraced in the steamy whirlpool. Nikki felt vulnerable as she laid her head on his chest. Nobody had ever fucked her that good before. She knew she was extremely attracted to Derrick but had no idea she would experience what had just taken place. Her pussy was still pulsating as she slid off his penis. "Damn nigga, so that's how you put it down" smiled Nikki trying to maintain her composure. I love you almost slipped off her lips and she knew that was a NO, NO . . . . "So whose good dick did I just have the pleasure of enjoying. I know it must belong to some lucky chick?"

"I don't have a girlfriend Nikki" smiled Derrick. "I haven't had time to commit" in a way Nikki was relieved to hear he was single, but also apprehensive because she wasn't quite ready to be in another relationship either. The last man she fell in love with got killed in a motor cycle accident. She swore she'd never feel that same way again about anyone at least until she met Derrick. It was something about him that reminded her so much of her ex. And even he had never fucked her the way Derrick just did. Yes Nikki was feeling very vulnerable right now . . . .

Derrick caught a cab from Nikki's condo early the next morning. As much as he wanted to stay he had to get home and check on his mom. Nikki had morning college classes at Coppin State college. She was a nursing major with expectations of becoming a nurse practitioner. She carried a GPA of 4.0 and was eligible for several scholarships. She was even recommended for medical school but declined. A Master's degree in nursing was all she aspired to obtain. Nikki had an unusual background to be a stripper, she came from a very professional family. Most the other girls had suffered a lot of hardships growing up that had forced them into that way of life; however, Nikki's father was a prominent surgeon at Johns Hopkins hospital and her mother a Registered Nurse. Nikki moved out of her parents beautiful 10 acre estate in Monkton, Maryland when she was sixteen. Her dad was very strict and she rebelled against his house rules. Dr. Brown was not born into wealth, he earned it and he set high expectations for Nikki and her older brother Carl who was gunned down in Baltimore city at the age nineteen. Carl had friends from the city and would hang out with them on the weekends. However on one particular Saturday morning he would never return home. Instead he would be shot dead standing on an East Baltimore corner by a bullet meant for someone else; a sad tragedy not uncommon on the City streets of Baltimore, Maryland; which earned it the name, Baltimore, Murdaland. From that day on Nikki wasn't allowed to go into the city and was forbidden to hang out with her girlfriends there. Nikki understood her father's grief and concern but, she also felt it was unfair for him to be so over protective.

She left home never to return and as far as her parents were concerned she had a 9 to 5 job working for a temp agency. If her parents knew she was a stripper they would be emotionally crushed. So she never bothered to tell them. Now at age twenty she was doing her thing. She had her own money, her own condo, and about to graduate from college with a Master's degree in nursing; Like NeYo and Jamie Foxx said, "SHE GOT HER OWN THING!"

CHAPTER 16

Derricks cab driver took St. Paul street to Martin Luther King Blvd. He stared out the window thinking about Nikki; how beautiful and intelligent she was. However the closer he got to his moms residence in Cherry Hill the more he felt a cloud of despair return. He paid the driver and exited his cab. Mrs. J's son was out front sweeping the sidewalk. "Yo what up Derrick, what's goin on man how you been. How's your mom?"

"Ok Rick, thanks for asking my brother. I'm bout to check on her again now" "Aight man if we can do anything to help let us know, we her OK" "Aight thanks" Derrick replied. Cherry Hill had a reputation of violence and crime, however many residents of The Hill stuck together and looked out for one another. The morals and values of the elders of the community were seen in the actions and attitudes of the youth. Some genuinely cared and showed respect for their neighbors. Derrick placed his key in his moms front door and turned the lock slowly as he began to sink back into a state of depression as he stood in the doorway listening to her cough, which sounded like a death rattle. Derricks mom was diagnosed with CHF, a debilitating heart condition which demanded her to have a heart transplant as soon as possibly.

Chronic heart failure meant her heart muscle wasn't pumping an adequate amount of blood and oxygen to her body. And if she didn't receive a heart transplant soon she would surely die. Derrick climbed the stairs slowly. He would usually sprint-up them two at a time. However today he was disappointed at the outcome of his fight. He could've used the winnings from the fight to help pay towards his moms operation. The rhythmical sound of her oxygen machine roared as it supplemented her body cells with oxygenated blood. Derrick forced himself to smile as he entered her room. He didn't want her to know he was upset. That would only make her more depressed. He pulled up a chair next to her bed and held her hand as he kissed her gently on the forehead.

Although she was extremely ill Derrick's mom had a smile that would brighten up a whole room of disparity. Her faith in God sustained her. And she would always reflect on the book of Job in the Old Testament of the Bible. Derrick's mom never smoked cigarettes, drank alcohol, or used drugs. Her disease was hereditary. She often wondered why her; but then came to the understanding of why not her. Life had a tricky way of following a certain pre-destined order, regardless of one's willingness, conscious awareness, and preparation." Some things just were, what they were" she could tell Derrick was upset and she knew about him losing the fight. It was on the evening news.

"Don't worry son" she said squeezing his hand with what strength she could muster. It's gonna be ok" your grandmother once told me many years ago before she died. "If you really want to make God laugh tell him what you got planned"

Derrick's mom was a very wise woman. However Derrick felt an obligation to provide for her by any means necessary. He too believed in God and was a very spiritual person, however today his faith would be tested and only God knows the outcome of the choices he would make in the next few days . . . .

CHAPTER 17

Derrick sat looking at the drug lords business card once more trying to decided which course of action he should take. By the time he got a rematch from Dennis Chapman his mom could possibly be dead. "Where else am I gonna get fifty grand?"

Derrick thought to himself. "The kickboxing match was my ticket and I got robbed. They know I won that fight. "Damn it!!" shouted Derrick. "I wanna do the right thing, but it seems my options are limited." At this point Derrick blamed God for his fate and misfortune. Why was his mother born with a debilitating heart condition and why was the damn fight fixed. Derrick's mind state of self-pity superseded his rationale. His emotional state was now driven by acceptance and anger; accepting the fact his mom was going to die unless she got the operation and angry with God for allowing such a good person to be so ill.

The paradox of the matter was that Derrick would pursue his final option, becoming the person he most despised. An enforcer for a drug Kingpin that contributed to the destruction of his fellow man supplying illicit drugs to the black community annihilating a generation of future doctors, lawyers, star athletes, and businessmen for ones own survival and greed. There was a small margin between right and wrong in a world of double standards and hypocrisy. "Is this it God? Am I supposed to be a gangster and a thug preying on the lives of others" Derrick's faith in God was diminishing and now he was going to do what he felt he had to do taking matters into his own hands. For the first time in life he would abandon his religious beliefs which taught him as a Christian to have faith and trust in God. And his philosophical training from martial arts which taught him to preserve and protect life and to destroy an opponent only in self-defense.

Deep inside he knew what he was about to do was wrong and that his affiliation with death and destruction would eventually come back to haunt him, leading to his own possible demise; it was inevitable. However Derricks mind was made up. It was time to take care of business and he was down for whatever. He would deal with the consequences when that time came. Derricks ability to adapt, lead, and execute plans of action would take him far; but how far was too far in a drug game that often came with a penalty of destruction and death to its perpetrators.

The following morning Derrick awoke around 6am he checked in on his mom to see if she was ok. She slept soundly as the sound of her oxygen machine hummed at 4liters of Oxygen a min via a humidifier. She appeared to be sleeping so he didn't disturb her.

Derrick commenced to perform his daily workout which consisted of muscle stretching and calisthenics before an intense martial arts workout and four mile run. Again Derricks internal dialogue transformed to a mind state of opposition and grief as he ran by the Cherry Hill shopping center where his good childhood friend Leon had been shot and killed and then by his old Jr. high school where his friend named Ernie had been gunned down fatally in the streets. The last quarter mile he exerted himself immensely as he sprinted; his clothes became saturated with perspiration. Derrick slowed his sprint to a fast paced walk to cool down as beads of sweat poured from his forehead evaporating into the cool August morning air. His heart rate was 140bpm and slowly declining to his normal resting rate of 60bpm after he cooled down. Fortunately for Derrick he didn't inherit his family's debilitating heart disease. Derrick arrived home around 7:30am His mom was now awake watching a news cap on The Fox 45 news channel. He took a quick shower and prepared her a low sodium, low cholesterol breakfast consisting of Oatmeal, two poached egg whites, and oat bran toast. With a small glass of OJ and non-fat milk.

Her lunch and dinner usually consisted of tuna salad or broiled chicken with mixed vegetables or a salad.

Derrick's loyalty and dedication to his mothers well being was endless being he was an only child, however she did have a younger sister who would also stop by to check on her after work. Her younger sister was married and had five kids of her own. But she still made time to check up on her big sis. After all they were the only two siblings growing up together and she was fortunate not to have any type of heart condition. Since his mom was classified as disabled she received Medicaid which appointed her a home nurse that came out to check on her three times a week. Derrick lived two blocks away from his mom in a room he rented for $75.oo a week which he paid with monies earned as a martial arts instructor at a local Dojo started by Sensei-T. Derrick became head instructor of the school when his Sensei became paralyzed. He would now turn the Dojo over to his fellow martial artists, Dino. Another skilled fighter with exemplary martial arts skills. Derrick knew once he became affiliated with Q's organization he would have to sever all ties with his Dojo and martial arts affiliates. He had great respect for his Dojo and his fellow martial artists. It was time to call Q. Their meeting was scheduled for the following Saturday . . . .

CHAPTER 18

It was 4:00 pm EST. For the last 30 minutes Derrick had been sipping fresh squeezed lemonade beneath a huge lime green umbrella, which shielded him from the sun. The temperature was 94 degrees and climbing. The weather forecast in Md. was estimated to reach a high of 95 degrees, fortunately it wasn't much humidity. A slight breeze could be felt periodically. More than half the pitcher of lemonade remained on the table. Derrick continued to sit at Q's lavish poolside patiently awaiting his arrival. Momentarily he entertained the thought of joining the group of tight bikini wearing swimmers waving enticingly for him to join them in the pool. So far he counted a total of nine beautiful women, who appeared to be of various ethnic groups from Black and White; to Latino and Asian. Yes it was quite a variety of eye candy to behold. And quite a temptation for Derrick who reminded himself he was here for business. However an invitation from Q to join the sexy bikini lustful desires would be different. One girl in particular caught his eye.

It was Nikki. And little did Derrick know he would be seeing a lot of her now that he was affiliated with Q. She gave him a smile and a wink as she leaned her head back in the water and began to back stroke demonstrating her awesome body that he got to know all to well a few nights ago.

"Damn shawty fine." He thought to himself returning her wink and a smile." "Did that cute guy just wink at you?" smiled Susan, one ofNikki's girlfriends in the pool. "what guy?" asked Nikki sarcastically knowing damn well she knew Derrick; but she didn't let on to her girlfriends she knew him. However Susan already knew. She could tell when Nikki was lying. "You bitch, you do know him!" she said jokingly, splashing water in Nikki's face. Nikki smiled looking over at Derrick once more as she submerged her body completely in the pool thinking about how good he'd fucked her just a few nights ago.

It was now 4:25p.m. Derrick was beginning to think maybe Q had forgotten about him.

But then again the only time Q stated was 3:30pm That was the time in which he instructed Derrick to be in front of the Baltimore Arena downtown on Baltimore and Howard St. where he had his disappointing kickboxing match a few weeks ago. There Q's limo would take Derrick to their place of meeting. "Shit yeah" Derrick thought to himself elated with an ambiguous smirk on his face. "I could sure get used to living like this." Derrick had class but could never afford to live a lavish lifestyle of luxury. He'd seen and read about such luxuries on T.V. and in magazines but never thought he would ever experience it personally. The ride to Q's immaculate and elegant estate which sat on 60 acres of beautiful farmland in Baltimore county off, of Greenspring Rd. was one Derrick would never forget. The limo passed through an electronic gate fence and traveled up a driveway which was approximately a quarter of a mile long surrounded by tall oak trees on both sides. The 60 acre estate also had a circular drive way in front. To the left of the circular driveway sat a parking pad with Q's toys, which consisted of exotic cars ranging from Ferraris, Bentleys, and Lambo's to an old school collection of 57 Chevy's and other intriguing muscle cars of the sixties and seventies. Altogether Derrick counted what had to be at least 15 cars. The guest parking lot was in the back. There he saw every car from Japanese imports like Lexus, Infinity's, and Nissan 300zx's; to Porsches, Mercedes, Jaguars, Range Rovers, and Cadillac's. All top of the line luxury models.

The mansion was covered in light tan sanded bricks and had a sash of beautiful Palladium windows. An array of exotic small palm trees imported from Hawaii outlined a spectacular aqua blue opal shaped pool. Other exotic plants and small trees stood impressively throughout the estate as well. The year of 1987 Q's estate was estimated to be worth at least $2,000,000.00 This same property would be worth at least $6,000,000.00 by 2010. Even during the great recession brought on by the tragedy of 911 in September 2001. When nineteen al Qaeda terrorist hijacked four commercial U.S. airlines and deliberately crashed them into The World Trade Center and the Pentagon, which not only devastated the city of New York, but the whole United States and The Global Market. The housing market in America would crumble with an epidemic of foreclosures that would rock the nation. Derrick felt lucky and like a privileged guest. All of Q's staff from drivers to bar maids treated him with the utmost respect and were ready to serve him. There were other people at the pool as well, many of whom Derrick assumed to be friends or associates of Q. So far Nikki was the only person he saw there he knew. Two seductive poised female waitresses wearing G-string bikini's paraded the pool ready to take drink and food orders and their personalities were as beautiful as their sexy bodies. Derrick maintained his composure as a gentleman with diplomacy. He reminded himself he was there for business, not pleasure. And little did he know he was being tested. Q purposely prolonged meeting with Derrick to see if he could be easily persuaded by the presence of a beautiful woman and in this case it was several of them. So far, Derrick was on point and was in Q's good favor. For some reason Derrick knew this so he decided to implement a little conservative fun.

He wanted to see if the two sexy bikini wearing waitresses were all show or would they serve him attentively as the two Caribbean dressed gentlemen sporting kaki shorts with expensive silk shirts half buttoned exposing their 14kt yellow gold Cuban linked chains which hung loosely from their necks. The two light complexioned gentlemen appeared to be of some Latin decent, however Derrick wasn't certain. He couldn't determine their nationality sitting so far away. They could just be two light skinned curly haired brothers. One thing was for certain, they were definitely there on business because they weren't easily distracted by all the lavish activities happening around them. One group of guest were smoking weed and another snorting coke and partying having a good time. However these two sat unamused holding on to their black duffle bags sipping their drinks. Before Derrick could complete his conservative hand gesture to the beautiful waitress on his left he was greeted by the one on his right. "So you decided to quench your thirst with something stronger than lemonade I see, what can I get you?" she was referring to the top shelf variety of alcoholic beverages inhabiting the bar.

Which contained every spirit imaginable. If Q's bar didn't stock it; it wasn't made.

Derrick was flattered by the beautiful, long legged, sun tanned, blonde haired, G-string bikini wearing God send standing before him about 5'9" tall. She leaned forward removing a napkin from her tray wiping it gently across Derricks face absorbing the sweat which beaded on his forehead. A childish grin formed his face as he looked into her seductive aqua blue eyes glancing momentarily at her pleasantly rounded size 38 DD's which fitted snuggly between her tight fitting bikini bra strap. Her nipples were erect as daisies at sunrise. Derrick maintained his composure and proceeded to answer her question. He couldn't determine if her double D's were all natural or silicon; regardless they were nice. "Humm let's see how about a spring water beautiful lady."

"You sure that's not too strong. Spring waters been known to have a bit of a kick you know" she said with a tone of sarcasm. She was now standing with an erect posture and Derrick's eyes captured each curvature of her sexy 38-22-36 body. She gotta a nice round phat ass for a white chick he thought to himself. She was definitely a site to behold. "I thought maybe you would like something with a little more kick to it."

"Kick?" Derrick said with a smile. "Well how about a sparkling water, that's got a little kick and fizz." She was amused at Derrick's quick wit and sense of humor.

"Oh I see, you're a wise guy" she said smiling. Walking away as her mesmerizing body projected an essence of precision strutting energetically over to the bar.

She knew all eyes were focused on her as she demonstrated her full capabilities.

Her long slender legs moved awesomely as her 38 DD's and round bodacious ass bounced in a rhythmical cadence sending a sensual, sexual synapse to everyone who dared participate in her exotic demonstration of optical fulfillment. Derrick knew Nikki was watching him, watch her and detected a slight bit of jealously. Nikki smiled at him sticking out her tongue. Derrick couldn't help but laugh. "You're alright girl." Derrick said to himself smiling back at Nikki. Nikki was the coolest of the cool though, it wasn't too much that could unnerve her. That's why Q loved having her in his presence.

Nikki wasn't phony or fake. She always kept it real and Derrick felt himself falling for her.

CHAPTER 19

The time was now 4:30 pm Q had seen enough. As far as he was concerned Derrick was ok, but he still had much to prove as far as, loyalty was concerned. Q along with his two cold blooded killing looking bodyguards that accompanied him in the limo the night of the fight approached the table. Derrick was beginning to think they were inseparable; everywhere Q went his two armed bodyguards followed with an intense look of murder in their eyes.

There was no telling how many men they had murdered for this flamboyant gangster who seemed to project a strong authority and an innate ability to lead and manipulate the minds of anyone he encountered with his blood monies, power, and persuasiveness. Q had the power of an army general and a brigade of loyal soldiers willing to kill at his command. Within two minutes the young sun tanned blonde boom shell returned with Derricks sparkling water. "Good afternoon Mr. Q" "Good afternoon Tracey, I see you've met my new business associate Derrick" "Yes sir, he's quite a charmer" she said standing with her awesome erect posture holding her tray in both hands. "Don't mind me, serve the gentleman his drink" "Certainly" she said displaying a beautiful captivating smile and sarcastic tone of voice. "Here you are Derrick one spring water with a kick" "With a kick?" remarked Q "It's a sparkling water Mr. Q" Tracey laughed. "Can I get you one?" "Now you know I require much more kick than that Tracey" "You can bring me my usual" "One Remy on the rocks coming up Mr. Q"

"Yeah that's got a couple kicks and punches" said Derrick as they all laughed. Except for the two bodyguards of course whose cold blooded expressions never changed. Q excused himself momentarily. "Be right back Derrick, got some quick business to tend too"

Escorted by his two fierce looking body guards Q walked diplomatically over to the table where the two Latin looking gentlemen were seated.

They were two Colombian drug runners employed by Q. They obtained Q's cocaine from drug carriers know as mules.

Today they each had twenty kilos. 88 pounds of pure fish scale cocaine which they carried concealed in two duffle bags. Q had a team of 50 deliverers that always traveled in pairs of two. Once they brought the coke in it was really no need to check for purity. It was always what it was supposed to be except for on occasion when a mule might get greedy and tried to cut the product, but the runners responsible for those particular mules would deal with them right then and there cutting off their hands which they would deliver to Q with whatever remained of the shipment and of course the mules would be executed with Colombian neckties; their throats slit and tongues pulled through their neck. Actually resembling a short necktie. That seldom happened though because no one was ever stupid enough to steal cocaine from Q. The penalty of death just wasn't worth it. Each week deliverers would rotate to alleviate suspicion of travel authorities. Whether by air, land, or sea Q and his Colombian cartel affiliates were determined to make their cocaine reach American soil; after all America was cocaine's billion dollar consumer. During his reign in the eighties Freeway Rick Ross was the number one supplier of cocaine endorsed by the CIA and The United States government. The streets of California would never be the same. Cocaine was a cash cow and everybody who was anybody cashed in and made millions of dollars during the eighties and nineties; from street hustlers to business men and corrupt politicians.

Q greeted his two runners in Spanish which he spoke fluently after years of doing cocaine business, most of which he learned from his mentor and late friend Rodriquez.

Both men stood exchanging greetings with Q in respect for his generous hospitality. The men where now all speaking English. Not all deliverers spoke English as fluently as these two, but most of the time at least one of the two paired Colombian drug runners would speak fluent English. Q waved his arm motioning for a young gentleman from his estate to come out and escort his two runners inside. A small office inside the mansion was where all final transactions would be made. Q's receiver would weigh the kilos, test the product, and pay the drug-runners who would receive

$10,000.00 for each kilo. Today's drop was a total of 40 kilo's, so the runners were paid $400,000.00 cash; each placing $200,000.00 back in their duffle bags. Q paid wholesale for his product and on the streets his drug lieutenants would sell retail doubling his money.

Street value, his Kilos would sell for $20,000.00 to $25,000.00 a pop to weight buyers.

His cocaine was pure fish scale and hard to come by so heavy hitters paid the price. Other product was broken down and sold in $1,500.00 ounces and $60.00 grams. On lower level operations glass Pyrex cookers would be used to rock up the cocaine and make a killing selling five, ten, and twenty dollar rocks making up to $3,000.00 off of one once;

Cut with a little B-12 and cooked with a little baking soda an ounce of fish scale cocaine could go a long way. Especially when hit with the ether.

Rock cocaine, aka ready rock was pioneered by Freeway Ricky Ross and Free basing was made poplar by none other than the famous and funny man Richard Pryor who was a legendary comedian who had a deadly encounter with smoking cocaine and survived to tell the story after almost burning himself to death. Of all the methods of using cocaine; freebasing proved to be one of the most addicting, marketable, profitable and deadly . . . . Killing a lot of its users regardless of their social status . . . .

CHAPTER 20

Q looked good for thirty-eight years old. He generated a healthy glow and solid stature of a man half his age and soon his daughter Tina would fall in love with a man who was just like her father: Self-sufficient, smooth, tall, dark, and handsome that would spoil her just like he did. Tina was only sixteen yrs. old and had the best of everything. From custom imports to the finest clothes and attended the best schools. It was ironic how she would meet and fall in love with Kilo who was really a nobody at the time. A nickel and dime hustler selling twenty dollar rocks on Jack and 10th St. in Brooklyn, Md. with a notorious hustler named Flava from Cherry Hill who was also about making money.

Kilo and Flav hustled from sun down to sun up often competing for the same customers but had mutual respect for each other. And that was unusual because Flava respected noone. Flav was such a gangster he once robbed a stash house where nigga's was sitting counting thousands of dollars. However, to add insult to injury he refused to wear a ski-mask out of GP because he wanted the dope boys to know who robbed them and dared them to do anything about it. Of his four man crew Flava remained unmasked. The Dope boys saw him on the strip and never said or did shit.

Flava was that kind of street certified hustler. He re-upped on coke with their dope money. Kilo and Tina meet at The Baltimore Inner Harbor. He was chillin with some of his goons from the streets spending money after selling drugs all morning and she was carousing Baltimore's number 1 tourist attraction with some of her girlfriends from private school. "Hello beautiful" Kilo spoke, after smoking weed and taking a few sips off a 40oz. of Old English. "Excuse me?" said Tina knowing damn well Kilo was addressing her. "Let's get something to eat" he said in response. Not knowing what the hell else to say. Tina was a beautiful young lady and looking at her real Gucci hand bag and expensive attire he knew she was pampered. Her designer bags and clothes didn't come from Canal St. ; they came from Manhattans, Saks Fifth Ave. Kilo knew someone had to be spoiling her. But he wanted it to be him. He feel in love with Tina at first sight "You need to come wit me to New York this weekend Shorty. Let me show you some things"

It was also love at first sight for Tina. And little did Kilo know even though he was two years older than her he'd finally met a girl that was time enough for his hustling ass.

Tina was beautiful, but street smart. Even at age sixteen she had a sexy ass body and stood about 5'4" tall and weighed about 115lbs. She had nice tits, a nice ass, and a pretty face. Yet and still what Kilo admired most was her wit. Tina wasn't the usual well kept, pretty, stuck-up chick that was all naive and easily impressed by a nigga wit money. After all her father was one of the biggest drug dealers to ever play the game and he made sure if a nigga ever wanted to impress his daughter he'd better come correct.

That's why he spoiled her with nothing but the best. Tina was a Gucci girl but she could also be shrewd and cunning. Many a hustler tried to impress her only to find themselves looking stupid after she'd played their ass. Spending all their money on her trying to be big shots trying to get some ass. And when they found out who her father was they dared not step to her; however Kilo was a true hustler. And he reminded her a lot of her father.

Over the next several years Kilo would become street certified; a mister untouchable.

Only few nigga s could run major operations on the street and not get popped. Especially with the number of good cops turned bad enticed by money, greed, and power using informants to give up drug dealers on the street to maintain their freedom and feed their addiction. These street rats would sell out their mother for a fix of dope or a hit of coke.

Kilo was born in New York City, but raised in Baltimore, so there wasn't too much he hadn't seen or done. But he was never a snitch.

CHAPTER 21

Q and Kilo were parallel in the drug game even though they ran drug empires in two different decades. Two drug kingpins separated by a few decades yet and still their M.O. and circumstances were much the same; however all things change. And so would the methods of operation in the drug game. Q was a multi-millionaire during the late seventies and eighties selling twenty to thirty kilos of cocaine a month during his reign.

During the late nineties and into the new millennium Kilo was selling hundreds of kilos of cocaine and heroin a month with shipments arriving two or three times a month via imports: air, land, and sea from Mexico, Colombia, and Afghanistan. He would pay electronically through Swiss accounts; legitimate business accounts laundering billions of dollars a year. These accounts were set up by Swiss bankers who would recruit hustlers and corrupt businessman by sponsoring lavish events in Florida.

Swiss recruiters would throw lavish parties to lure in its financial playas. They would use encrypted lap tops to hide their American clients accounts, which contained millions and billions of dollars which remained off the radar from the United States governments, IRS.

In 2007, a Swiss banker named, Berkinfield and a whistle blower revealed over nineteen-thousand corrupt accounts to the United States government.

By the time of Kilo's incarceration in 2004 he was worth over a billon dollars on the streets and had millions stashed in Swiss accounts. A lot for a young nigga born in New York and raised in the Cherry Hill projects earning his stripes on the streets of Baltimore's Murdaland. Home of "The Wire" where only the strong survived and snitches died. There was much more loyalty amongst drug dealers during Q's reign in the seventies. In the eighties and nineties the judicial process was more severe on drug dealers, especially those dealers selling rock cocaine which carried a mandatory twenty year sentence; compared to powder cocaine dealers, who would receive a much lesser sentence. "Crack Laws" by the turn of the new millennium wanna be drug dealers were selling each out every second they could to maintain their freedom or setting each other up to be robbed for drug money. Trust and loyalty amongst dealers was replaced with snitches and grimy hustlers willing to sellout their best friend and comrade to save their own asses; or line their own pockets with blood monies. They would kill you as fast as they would say hello. There was no remorse. And no honor amongst thieves. Because now the code was GREED. The code of LOYALTY, from the old school hustlers from the seventies and early eighties like Q was fading fast. Hustlers were still grimy in the seventies but by the mid-eighties and on they was snitching like bitches; as matter of fact a lot of chicks was goin harder than the dudes not cracking under pressure.

CHAPTER 22

Q and Derrick sat at the pool side sipping their drinks. Derrick drank only half of his sparkling water while Q was ready for another Remy on the rocks. Q looked at Derrick knowing he'd made a good choice in allowing him into his circle. Derrick would be a strong link in the chain of lieutenants of his hierarchy. He had great expectations for him.

However Derrick had to prove himself worthy of such authority. "You are wise to take me up on my offer" Q's tone of voice became more authoritative although he maintained a calm demeanor. "I can definitely use a man like you in my organization." Q always spoke with complete confidence. His tone and pitch were very smooth and deliberate.

But, when angered he could be very intimidating. His whole demeanor would change. For the most part he possessed the calmness of a Zen master or a poised gentleman. But for real; Q was a cold blooded killer. "I'm also very aware of the fact that your primary motive is to earn monies for your mom's heart operation. I commend you for that young blood. And it's gonna all be taken care of. As long as you work for me your mother will receive the best medical treatment available" Derrick detected the sincerity in Q's voice. And for some strange inclination he felt like everything would be ok; yet he still he felt like he was making a deal with the devil.

Derrick was about to enter a point of no return. Q was in every essence a gangster and he lived by the code and creed that made men; made men. Like that of the Italian gangster code. It was, "Death before dishonor" Q was square when it came down to business, because he knew he would kill any man that crossed him and in turn he would die with that same honor if sought on for revenge by any man he'd ever crossed. These were his rules of engagement in the drug game. It was his way of life; his creed. It was this type of loyalty, honesty, drive, and commitment that separated soldiers from generals, foot soldiers from kingpins, and everyday workers from CEO's of multi-million dollar corporations. Q was a calculative mastermind and a natural business man. Much like that of Freeway Ricky Ross. Out of L.A. A true street certified hustler.

Q's social affiliations ranged from prominent doctors, savvy lawyers, and sophisticated political officials. Many of whom had no idea of his corrupt provocation. They were blinded by his many contributions to humanity and involvement in social and political events not knowing he was a cold blooded gangster. Q was notorious but remained a mystery to his affiliates. All they knew was he had money, and lots of it . . . Kilo on the other hand was raw and ruthless. He lived for today; fuck tomorrow. He tried to maintain a low profile but after the media coverage during his trial and incarceration he was now in the lime light and didn't give a fuck. Kilo was so well connected it didn't matter; this kid was making billions of dollars and little did he know he and his drug dealing conglomerates had stimulated the economy more than any stimulus bill ever could. It was the new millennium and Kilo and his crew were making mint and a lot of street certified hustlers rich; men and women.

It was a new generation of hustlers and money talked more than ever. It was survival of the fittest, and everyone took as much as they could, as fast as they could get it. From street hustlers to corporate executives. Morals became secondary to money. Why because it was a recession and the value of the American dollar was fading fast. And the only movers and shakers were hustlers getting money from Ponsey schemes, Hedge fund scandals, Inside trading on the stock market, Mortgage companies sucking consumers bank accounts dry, and Drug dealers on top of their game getting money while they still could. It was survival of the slickest; Whatever's clever . . . . "The sky was the limit!!" but many would crash and burn . . . .

CHAPTER 23

Most of Q's guest and business associates were gone. The remaining of his friends would be sleeping in guest quarters. It was now twelve-midnight. The chemistry between Nikki and Derrick was more intense than ever. She was lying face down on a beach chair with her ass cheeks smiling through her bikini G-string like two half moons.

Her ass almost looked like it was glistening as she reached forward removing a blunt from her purse. "Damn!" Derrick thought to himself. "This bitch got the most perfect ass, I've ever seen. No wonder she was one of the top paid and desired strippers on the block"

Many a lustful desirer had busted a nut to the sight of Nikki's mesmerizing bodacious ass from a far. Because that would be as close as they would come to cumming; in their fucking hands. Horny mother fuckers would pay a grip to stick their dick in her pussy for one minute if she'd let them. Instead Nikki would sell them a wet dream while emptying their pockets. She was a true certified hustler. Derrick smiled as he sat on the side of the beach chair palming her left ass cheek in his right hand. Nikki's G-string was saturated with wetness. It was just something about this nigga made her want to fuck.

She'd never felt this way about any man and it scared her. Nikki lit her blunt with a lighter, taking two puffs passing it to Derrick. He hesitated initially remembering where he was, but shit . . . business was done and he was on his own time now. If he wanted to smoke a little weed with a fly ass chick, that was his own business. Derrick took one puff.

"This some different shit shawty!" He said passing the blunt back to Nikki. "You like it?" she said smiling. Knowing damn well this was some true fire shit. An exotic blend of weed from Hawaii that you would never find on the streets. Shit that put the bass in LOUD!! Nikki took another puff sitting up on the beach chair. "Come here nigga." Nikki said pulling Derrick's chin as she kissed him gently on the lips. Derrick took two more puffs of the blunt, blowing the remaining smoke in Nikki's face. She knocked the blunt from his hand and stood up pressing her large breast in his face.

Derrick kissed her lips gently while unsnapping the draw string of her swim suit. Her size 38 breast stood firm and erect as he slid his tongue down to her nipples.

Derrick began licking her nipples and sucking her tits. "Oh Gawd!!" Nikki sighed.

Derrick pulled Nikki into his arms tongue kissing her passionately. "OH shit!" she said sliding down Derrick's Adidas sweat suit pants grabbing all eight inches of his dick, which was rock hard. "Fuck me nigga!" Nikki slid down her G string bikini to her ankles as she turned her back to Derrick. Derrick pulled her close to his erection sliding his dick up placing it between her big perfectly round ass cheeks. The tip of his dick throbbed against her lower back. Nikki leaned forward grabbing Derricks dick pulling it slowly into her wet pulsating pussy as he bent her over a white pool chair. Derrick pulled back and then thrust forward gently pulling her hips toward him as he slid deeper inside her hitting her G spot. Nikki's head snapped back as she sighed with pleasure bouncing her perfectly round ass up and down as Derrick slid deeper inside her love zone. Derrick felt like he was gonna explode and Nikki could feel it. She had already cum twice herself.

Pussy juices streamed down her thighs. "OH SHIT!!" sighed Derrick as his knees buckled feeling her wetness. He Grabbed her beautiful round ass once more as he thrust deep inside her pulsating pussy. They both collapsed on the chair panting momentarily, exhausted from their romantic interlude. "Damn nigga you know how to put it down" smiled Nikki gathering her things. Derrick raised his hand and swiftly smacked her on the ass. Nikki loved it." Do it again daddy, you know just what I like" "Freak"

Derrick said smiling. "Takes one to know one" Nikki responded sarcastically.

They both laughed. The effects of the exotic weed and the excitement they experienced fucking had them in a mental state of euphoria. Derrick pulled up his sweat pants as Nikki grabbed him by the hand and escorted him back to her sleeping quarters. Most of the girls had their own room on the left wing of Q's spacious 14 bedroom estate. Nikki's room had its own bathroom, she and some of the other dancers and barmaids would often reside there for the summer. Q loved surrounding himself with beautiful women. And he only kept people around him whom he felt he could trust. He was like the black Hugh Hefner with his own playboy mansion. Derrick and Nikki made love the whole night.

Even though they knew it was undeniable chemistry between them they made no commitments. Tonight would be their last one together and the last time they would see each other again for a long time. Derrick had business down in VA to attend for Q. This would be Derricks first drug deal. He would accompany two of Q's drug runners down to Virginia beach to drop off two kilos of cocaine to a major buyer in Portsmouth.

Q had many clients he supplied throughout the United States and did so for a generous fee of $5,000.00 or more depending on the distance and risk factor. If his buyers met at a halfway point fees were less. And of course if they came to Baltimore there were no additional fee's and his birds would fly for about $20K Q only dealt in weight supplying street dealers with the best cocaine on the market. He never sold less than a brick.

Anything less than a Kilo was a waste of time. He'd let the street dealers sell the ounces.

Derrick was quite apprehensive his first drug run; however most of his stress and tension was produced from the guilt and shame he internalized due to the nature of his affiliations and actions. But Derrick was loyal and he was prepared to do whatever he had too to ensure his moms well being making sure she got the heart operation she needed. Q kept his word and expedited Derricks mom heart transplant. She was immediately hospitalized and given the best medical care permissible. Derrick was apprehensive about leaving his mom because he was always there for her but, Q assured him she would receive the best medical care available and that no medical procedure would be performed unless it was absolutely necessary until his return from Va. He would be in Va. for no more than one or two days. That would give them ample time to cross and type possible donors and fortunately his mom had a universal blood type 0+. All Derrick had to do was protect Q's drugs and money.

CHAPTER 24

Virginia Beach was the meeting spot. The time was 6:30pm and the August sun was just beginning to set. The air was kinda of cool near the water off the boardwalk. Despite his initial nervousness Derrick displayed nothing but utter confidence as he walked a few feet to the left of the gunner. They were three paces behind the courier who carried the two kilos of coke.

The gunner packed a Glock 9mm which he was trained to shoot. Gunner was an ex-cop turned crooked and kicked off the squad due to his criminal affiliations.

He was a conflict of interest to law enforcement and an asset to Q's organization.

Derrick's eyes scanned the beach intensely looking for any possible under-covers and Stickup boys. The transaction was easier than he anticipated. For some reason he thought it would be more complicated. The buyer and courier met at a pier and exchanged duffle bags. It was understood neither party would depart until the other checked their money and or the product. The buyer also had two armed enforcers that watched his back in case some one brought them a move. Upon completion of the deal each party exited as discreetly as they arrived. This was one of the easier runs. Q wanted to get Derrick familiar with making drug deals even though he knew he was street smart and capable of taking care of himself. The likely hood of being brought a move from Narc's or stick up boys was ill to none. The conversation back to Baltimore was no more interesting then the one to Virginia. Derrick's new drug dealing colleagues weren't much for conversation with someone they just met even though Q validated him. Which was fine with Derrick because he wasn't one who engaged a lot in small talk. He judged people by their actions because from his experience people often embellished themselves with their words and egos and he was quick to read fake, snake mother fuckers who liked to bluff.

As soon as Derrick got back to Baltimore he visited his mom at Harbor View Hospital.

Everything was set. Her operation was scheduled for Monday at 6:30 am The next 72 hours were the most exhausting Derrick had experienced in a long time, however his mother's operation was a success. The next few days she would spend recovering. For Derrick it was time to get back to business selling cocaine for Q.

18 months had passed and Derrick was now one of the crew. Drug runs to Va. were now more relaxed and Gunner and the courier were much more comfortable with Derrick.

Between runs they would hang out in Norfolk and Portsmouth at night clubs like the Main Event and Club David's on High street; A military club with a lot of fine females.

After all Portsmouth and Norfolk were military towns and they would often encounter a lot of major players from New York, Philly, D.C., and Baltimore. Many of whom were enlisted in the military, tri state hustlers making major moves from to state to state.

Even a lot of hustlers from the Midwest got in on the action from Detroit and Chicago.

Street certified hustlers making major cash; selling everything from guns to needles to cocaine and heroin. Some weekends they would even party with rich college kids from the Hamptons. The Foxes Den in Portsmouth was also a popular spot to unwind.

CHAPTER 25

Two years had passed before Derrick and Nikki saw each other again and a lot had changed. Subsequently to their reuniting Nikki completed her college courses obtaining her master's degree in nursing. Which she didn't have any need for because she was now the love interest of Big R. Q's under boss and a major player in the drug game.

Big R stood about 6'0 tall and weighed about 300 pounds. Even though he was big he was clean and stayed wearing nothing but the best of imported fabrics from Italy. Q would often tease him calling Big R the black Italian because he wore nothing but the best leather Italian shoes which complimented his tailored suits and shirts. Big R was a clean shaven caramel complexioned brother with a scar under his left cheek which flawed his otherwise pretty boy appearance. Big R got that scar from a street fight many years ago when his assailant missed his eye by inches with the slash of straight razor. Of course his razor swinging assailant was killed by Big R who beat him senseless and slit his throat with his own straight razor. He stood over his dying victim and dared anyone to call the police or an ambulance. Big R was a ruthless killer. Quarts of blood oozed from the throat of his bleeding victim who rolled on the ground squealing like a pig that was just slaughtered. Bystanders stared in disbelief as he died covered in a pool of his own blood. From that day on everyone called him Razor, which later became Big R.

Big R was a major asset to Q's organization representing him mostly in the Midwest overseeing most of the drug shipments to Detroit and Chicago. He had a pass in the projects because of his affiliation with the B.G.D and Vice Lords. Big R didn't get caught up in sets. He was a cocaine dealer and kept his buyers supplied with nothing but the best YAYO . . . . Big R and Nikki dated on and off for a few months; he was ten years older than her and was known to impress the ladies with his lavish life style and he spoiled Nikki with crazy ice and nothing but the best of imported Italian fabrics, shoes and LV hand bags. She was flabbergasted when he proposed to her placing a 5kt flawless diamond set in a Platinum band on her finger. Big R pulled in about 6 figures every six months and hustled long enough to have a net worth of about 10 million. So when he proposed to her and promised her the world she fell head over heels; Big R literally swept Nikki off her feet. And she was no easy catch. Many a hustler would give anything to have her on their arm. Big R treated her like a princess, but little did she know 4 months after their fairy-tale wedding her prince charming would turn into a ugly frog treating her like a peasant. His loving, caring, and compassionate demeanor transformed into a self-centered and egotistical raving lunatic. Almost every Friday night he would entertain his drug lieutenants at his home playing poker boasting and bragging about men that crossed him and how he killed them in an abandoned warehouse. His favorite story was his six inch beauty scar on his left cheek and how he slit the throat of the man that gave it to him.

He boasted about how he watched his coward ass assailant bleed, squealing like a pig begging for someone to save him until most of his blood and life left his body. Big R used a straight razor cutting him ear to ear, severing his carotid artery. At peak levels of intoxication after too much cognac and too many lines of coke he would boast of how he made love to Nikki and how good she was in the bed, like it was any of their business. Many a Friday night she would sit at the top of the stairs of their immaculate $800,000.00 home in Owings Mills curled up like a baby lying on the floor in her night gown wishing she were dead. How did her life come to this. A sexy ass diva that men would kill for to being some bitch ass egotistical maniacs sex object. How could he degrade her like that after putting her so high on a pedestal making her feel like the most beautiful woman in the world. The love she thought she felt for him was turning quickly into hate.

Chapter 26

Derrick was excelling quickly in the drug game making a name for himself, earning much respect from his colleagues. Just a week ago on a drug run to Philadelphia to drop off six bricks for $120K Derrick demonstrated just how deadly he was. The transaction should've been easy. Deliver six kilo's to drug runners for a regular buyer at $20,000.00 a Kilo; collect $120,000.00 and be out; however today the runners where on the take.

Purchasing the coke was not an option because they already fucked up the buy money. In every drug cartel there are weak links and today was no exception. The drug runners were fuck ups and had no intentions of turning over the coke to their boss because they had already fucked up the buy money feeding their own crack head addictions. They were far beyond the savior of any serenity prayer and death would be their penalty; the point of no return. A fate derived by many hustlers that thought they were an exception to the rules of engagement in the drug game. Derrick could tell something wasn't right. This deal felt different. The attitudes and demeanor of the drug runners were suspect and their intentions of taking the six kilos of cocaine without paying was evident. Derrick could feel it; their smiles were resilient and bogus and as a counterfeit hundred dollar bill. Derrick kept his composure seeing through their bullshit. He stood with his hands behind his back with the keen observation and aptitude of a ninja assassin on a mission.

The finger-tips of his leather gloved right hand grazed lightly and slowly over the mahogany led filled nun-chuck fastened behind his lower back with a Velcro-strap.

His leather gloved left hand remained relaxed as he gently positioned his fingers on the tips of a throwing star. These six point razor sharp stainless steel stars had the ability to penetrate two-inch thick boards and cement blocks when executed by a trained martial artist and Derrick was one of the best.

Derrick studied the intended buyers eyes attentively detecting their nervousness and deceptive demeanor. It was something more than the cold February morning air that disturbed them. Everyone shivered involuntarily from the 27 degree weather except for Derrick. He was too pumped with adrenaline and his killer instinct was at its peak level.

The two drug buying prospects standing before him were about to experience utter and complete annihilation. Gunner posted himself to the left side of the courier who held the black leather duffle bag containing the 6 kilos of raw fish scale. Derrick posted himself to the right of the courier making sure he was in striking distance of the drug runners. The five men stood face to face on a deserted South Philly school playground, looking like rival gunman from the old west about to shoot it out at the OK corral. "How bout we get this shit over with, it's cold as shit out here" stated the courier. Unzipping the leather duffle bag revealing the six Kilos of cocaine. "Aight that's whut's good nigga!" responded the runner holding a black backpack, which he sat on the playground. Derrick was right in his presumption these two niggas were grimy and had no intentions of making a buy. At that moment the runners partner lifted his black full length peacoat in revealing a sawed off shot gun.

Derrick responded without hesitation. He knew it wasn't $120,000.00 coming out from under the peacoat. Besides usually the person carrying the loot would reciprocate by revealing the buy money not sit it on the ground. Derrick snatched his nun-chucks from the Velcro-strap fastened to his lower back. The motion of his arm forward and flick of his wrist amplified the momentum of this deadly martial arts weapon; which were two 10" mahogany, led filled sticks, 2 ½ inches in diameter, linked by a 8 inch chain secured by a swivel. This lethal martial arts weapon resembled a toy of some type, however in retrospect was created as a gardening tool during the era of ancient China to beat down weeds and ward off insects. Ancient Chinese martial artists cultivated its use as a deadly martial artist weapon. The craze of this lethal and deadly weapon swept Western America and was demonstrated by masters of the art of fighting like Bruce Lee, Dan Inosanto, and Jim Kelly of the silver screen. Karate schools throughout the United States incorporated the lethal nun-chunk as a martial arts weapon and Derrick mastered the skill of its use.

The swinging motion of his arm extended, as he swirled the nun-chuck gripped firmly in his right hand. The extended end of the lethal weapon smashed against the intended runners face producing a cracking sound which echoed the playground, breaking his jaw bone upon impact. He let out a painful agonizing cry as his arms went limp and the shot gun fell aimlessly to the ground.

The other drug runner attempted to assist his partner, but was not quick enough for Derricks martial arts skills and lightning quick speed. A back spin kick was followed up by Derrick's use of the nun-chucks once more, this time splitting the other runners head open like a ripe coconut. "Damn!" Responded Gunner as he looked at the courier. "This nigga bad as shit, Yo!" they were astonished at Derricks lightening quick speed and lethal technique. Derrick had taken them both out before Gunner or the courier could ever get a shot off. Just out of GP. Gunner shot both of them anyway.

POP . . . POP . . . POP . . . POP . . . POP . . . POP . . . rang off his Glock 9mm. til both me were lying motionless bleeding helplessly on the ground. "This ain't no game niggas!" "Let's get the fuck outta here" said the courier to Derrick and Gunner. The following Drug runs for the dynamic trio were less complicated. Word was out these dudes weren't to be played wit. And if you crossed them your ass was like grass cut down by a John Deere mower on a Monkton farm.

CHAPTER 27

A year had passed. Derrick, Gunner, and the courier were top earners making major moves and Q a very rich man. Q ranked high amongst many major drug dealers in Baltimore, Md. and stayed off the radar. Still there were many young ambitious hustler's on the come up making their mark in the drug game falling victim to their own demise; one by one. Hustlers Greed was contagious . . . .

One year and six months in the drug game, Derrick was beginning to make a name for himself. He was accumulating a lot of money, as well as his street credibility. He was averaging about 4 to 6 runs a month making 2G's a run. and two thousand dollars for a day's work wasn't bad compared to what he made working at the Karate school. There it would've taken him two months to make two thousand dollars. Or any legal paying job for that matter. The saying, "It was no money like drug money." held much truth; and the consequences could be devastating. Not many hustlers remained immune from the fate of the DEA or the FEDs. Unless they had inside connects like Q had.

And he paid top dollar to corrupt cops and politicians to stay on top of his drug empire.

The import of drugs ironically seemed to stimulate the economy. Making everybody monies: from drug dealers, to the criminal justice system, to elaborate institutions that transformed drug money into big real estate ventures creating jobs for construction companies; even the common worker trying to earn a decent salary to feed his family. It was ironic how illegal drugs transformed dead beat towns into multi million dollar tourist spots like: Miami, Florida where cocaine pioneers of the seventies that put Florida on the map, making it a number one tourist and vacation spot bring in millions of dollars in revenue; all from drug monies and a little ingenuity.

Q was growing very fond of Derrick. He demonstrated great loyalty and ruthlessness in his drug organization as a future lieutenant and had the potential to one day be a possible under boss, which intimidated Big R. Q and Big R had hustled together since the late seventies with the induction of the movie, "Super fly" The # 1 drug dealing movie of that time. Which demonstrated the power and ingenuity of true street hustlers.

Similar to that of Scarface in the eighties and New Jack City in the nineties. Q and Big R had stomped much ground together and saved each other's lives many times from drug deals gone bad. And even on deals gone good when they'd made so much money and snorted so much cocaine they could've died if one or the other hadn't intervened. That was the nature of the business. And money was flowing like knowledge to the Pharos s of ancient Egypt. But it was rare when you could find a comrade that would ride or die for you. Most nigga's would always be out for self. If they got popped and the Feds threatened to give them time, they would sell out their grandma' ma to cop a plea deal. Pussy ass hustler's with no true loyalty to themselves or the drug game. Q's fondness and confidence in Derrick was growing rapidly. Derrick demonstrated the true dedication of a real hustler. He always remained loyal to Q's organization.

CHAPTER 28

Q's admiration and trust in Derrick was beginning to create much jealousy and animosity amongst his fellow comrades especially those who had been in Q's criminal organization for many years seeking to win his trust and confidence in them. Q only allowed the best of the best to take on a position of authority in his inner circle. His inner circle of organized crime affiliates took an oath sealed with blood. Those chosen would have to sacrifice 5 milliliters of blood. These select few would be honored like members of a secret society. "Til death do them part" the 5mls of blood surrendered represented a part of their physical being; like the bloodshed and slaughter of an animal during a religious ceremony. However, Q's initiation was merely a symbolic representation of trust and loyalty to his drug family and held no religious connotations. Yet those that knew Q symbolized the syringe with his deceased mom and her OD on heroin. All members who were elected and sacrificed blood held the power and prestige of a Mafia Don. They would be considered made man and couldn't be disrespected or killed by a fellow member unless authorized by Q. Nonetheless Forces of nature driven by jealousy and greed remained omnipotent and still thrived even within Q's inner circle. And his number one guy would soon betray him.

The year was 1990 and Q was holding his annual Christmas party at his exclusive estate in North West Baltimore. The party was one Q held every year for members of his inner circle and guest. And the first Derrick would attend not being officially initiated into the inner circle. This was the tenth year for Q's exclusive party and the first time someone not officially in the inner circle attended. But that's only because Q had intentions of initiating Derrick January the 1ST of 1991 which was in 6 days. Derrick was as good as in. Q held him at great esteem and had great confidence in his loyalty and dedication to his organization. Urban sectors across Maryland and its surrounding counties showed illustrious dedication to this traditional holiday called Christmas. From north to south and east to west; city projects to rural homes and estates in the county, all put forth an earnest effort to decorate their apartments and homes with Christmas bulbs, wreaths, and ornaments in attempt to capture and be a part of the Christmas spirit. Q's impressive estate which sat on 60 acres was no exception. Q took great pride in having his estate decorated for all the holidays, especially Christmas.

Christmas was always the time he saw people getting together with a bond of closeness and affection. Something he never had the opportunity to experience as a youth. As a kid he would watch an old black and white 13 inch T.V. in the back of the pool hall.

Unfortunately the "Leave it to Beaver" episodes he watched on the old black and white Zenith was far from the reality he experienced living as a youth, abandoned by his young mom and taken in by a pool hall hustler that taught him the rules of survival on the city streets of L.A. at the impressionable age of ten. Q would sit and stare for hours at the flashing Christmas bulbs. Blinking on and off illuminating the dark night with colors of red, white, blue, and green which reflected off of everything that came within a foot of its existence. It was something about the flashing lights that warranted Q's undivided attention. The strong flashing lights always made him feel safe. Protected from the surrounding evils that thrived within the walls of the naked city, which seemed to claim a life as frequent as one was being born. This was a feeling not uncommon to many urban youth growing up in the concrete jungle called the ghetto. From Baltimore, Murdaland to South Central L.A., boroughs of New York City and many other urban sector of America, black youth were being exposed to poverty, death and genocide. With living standards often experienced by those in third world countries. Could this really be happening in the rich land of America; the land of freedom, opportunity, and abundance.

Unfortunately, the American dream had become an American nightmare for many of this era. Success was what you made it; by any means necessary.

Q's moral fibers were exemplified and driven by a code of survival. As with many resilient ambitious hustlers and gangsters like Al Capone during the 1920's and 1930's with the alcohol prohibition and the ingenious efforts of bootleggers attempting to get a piece of the American dream by way of providing a service for what was in popular demand. Tobacco, alcohol, and drugs were always cash cows and big business in America. Regardless of the devastation and detrimental ramifications caused by tobacco, alcohol, and drugs, as long as they were made available someone was going to buy them.

CHAPTER 29

The Christmas night evening air was bitter cold. It was 10:30pm and guest were still arriving. The 30 degree temp. outside had no bearing on the 80 degree temp radiating within Q's illustrious estate. The men were dressed in after six tuxedos and the women wore expensive Italian evening dresses. It looked like an evening at the Oscars. The only thing missing was the red carpet. This particular event was reserved for black prestigious urban gangsters in Q's perilous crime family exemplifying another year in a drug trade that never promised tomorrow. Because for many attending, tomorrow wasn't promised.

Even though they were connected and worked above the level of the average street hustler, they were still not immune from the plagues of death that summoned a drug dealer to his fate. Whether it be life in prison or death: money, greed, and power bestowed a universal language that never required much cause for interpretation.

It's alluring addiction and passion would always remain eminent. Junkies weren't the only ones falling victim to the demeanor of the drug game. The allurement of financial freedom and social prestige were enough to make any young boy or man with a desire to make it out of the belly of poverty take a chance getting in the drug game selling cocaine and heroin, however only few survived this game. Even though many became incarcerated, even more lost their lives for being at the wrong place at the wrong time, not knowing what the hell they were getting into. The odds of survival were just as bad as a soldier on the front line of a war; Hopeless! Even with crossing all the T's and dotting all the I's one could still get it. Death has always been an equal opportunity entity that everyone would eventually meet. No matter how much money one had or didn't have; It was inevitable.

All eyes were on Derrick as he gunned his candy apple red Turbocharged Nissan 300zx up Park Heights enroute to Q's estate. He maxed the 3.0

liter, four cam, 24 valve engine. Which pushed out 300 horse power with precision. Derrick arrived at the party around 11pm most of Q's guests were already there. Derrick was wearing a black after six Nino Cerruti tuxedo with a red cummerbund that complimented his sporty red 300zx. He'd abandoned his usual attire for this evenings event. Which usually consisted of a Adidas sweat suit and sneakers. Tonight Derrick looked like he was about to walk down the red carpet. Q wanted nothing but the best for his big Christmas parties and tonight was no exception. That's why he hired one of Baltimore's most talented and demanded emcees to host this evenings event. DJ Frank Ski, from Baltimore's radio station V-103 was known to make any party a huge success with his crafty turntable skills and ability to rock the crowd. Frank Ski was the pulse of the air waves and always kept the party jumping. Derrick could feel the eminent energy flowing through the room as soon as he entered the door. The floor was filled with everyone getting their groove on dancing to Kurtis Blow's Christmas song. Everyone was partying and having a good time. Derrick was soon greeted by Q and introduced to other prominent figures in his drug organization. Everyone had fun and partied galore . . . .

"This is Derrick" stated Q introducing him to Big R. "So this the lil nigga that's been kicking ass from Baltimore to VA" joked Big R. "Looks kinda puny to me to be a fighter" everyone laughed at Big R's wise crack. "No seriously, welcome to the family Derrick, I been hearing a lot about you. If Q says you're a stand up guy. Well, you're a standup guy" Big R moved to the side revealing Nikki who stood quietly behind him.

"Oh yeah and this sexy ass chick is my wife, Nikki" a lump formed in Derrick's throat as Nikki smiled at him blushing. She couldn't bring herself to look Derrick in the eyes. A nervous tension seemed to fill the air. "What the fuck you too know each other or something?" smirked Big R. With a tone of sarcasm. "As a matter of fact they do" Q intervened. He could tell shit was about to get ugly. Big R was extremely jealous and possessive over Nikki even though at times he treated her like shit. "They both attended a pool party I had a few years ago. What was it 1987, 88 Derrick?

That's when you first started working for me" "Damn time flies." remarked Big R.

"Funny we never met before. I always heard about you like you was some living legend" everyone laughed again at Big R's sarcastic remark. "Damn!" Derrick thought to himself. Nikki was looking spectacular.

She was truly the most beautiful woman in the room in his eyes. She flaunted a long black evening dress designed by, Valentino. The dress fit Nikki to perfection showing off her gorgeous figure in her sexy, 38-24-36 5'5" frame.

She looked liked like a teenager standing next to Big R who was humongous in height and weight. Frank Ski slowed down the tempo, as he put Baby Face's, Whip Appeal on the turntable. Big R grabbed Nikki by the hand and pulled her close.

"Excuse me gentleman." Time to get my groove on" Derrick and Q nodded in response. "Thanks Q, I had a lost for words" "Yeah, I know nigga, Shatt!" laughed Q.

"Nikki tends to have that affect on most men. "I know you and her had a little encounter back in the day. She told me about it. And truth be told, she was getting feelings for you. And you the first nigga I ever seen her catch feelings for. Between me and you let what happened between you and Nikki stay in the past. My man Big R worships the ground she walks on, even though he treats her grimy sometimes"

Derrick wanted to know more, but decided to leave well enough alone. How could anyone ever mistreat anyone as kind and beautiful as Nikki. But as fate would have it Derrick would soon see. As the hour grew later and the party intensified with every spin of the turn table so would Big R's outlandish and obnoxious behavior when he had too many lines of cocaine and drank too much cognac.

Frank Ski was mixing Spoonie Rap on the turn table. And everyone was partying and having a good time. Nikki was dancing on the floor alone, looking as tempting as a sheep to a coyote. Her sexy body gyrated in a seductive and mesmerizing rhythm that always made her desirable; leaving onlookers spell bound like a snake charmer to a deadly rattler. Derrick and Nikki both smiled at each other as their eyes made contact and were spellbound as they both admired how good they both looked. Simultaneously their minds transcended to intimate moments they once shared together. It was like a little secret just between the two of them of how they fucked each other's brains out each time they were together alone. Time seemed to stand still as their eyes continued to meet 15 feet away. For that moment they both felt like they were the only ones in the crowded room. Derrick stood motionless as his stomach churned with butterflies, it was like the adrenaline rush he'd feel before every big fight. However this nervous tension and encounter was much different. He wanted to move towards her but couldn't. It was like he was trying to run in a dream, but was bound by some supernatural force that prevented him from moving. A few seconds seemed to turn into minutes during their lustful gaze.

No sooner than he could blink the inevitable happened. The sound of Big R's roar echoed the room as he snatched Nikki from the dance floor. "Bitch I ought to knock your head off" he swore. Looking like a big bear about to devour his victim.

Derrick's first instinct was to intervene, but he was quickly stopped by Q who grabbed him by the arm. "Don't do it Derrick. Let it go" he said. Knowing that Derrick was about rip Big R's head off. "What you like that nigga, I saw yall making fucking goo-goo eyes at each other" "You want to fuck him or something?" Big R was out of order.

Q walked over in attempt to make him chill. No one else had a chance of getting close when he was this high and aggravated. Q was the only one he would listen too. "Chill out nigga" he said in a discreet tone of voice, so only Big R and Nikki could hear. "Lil young blood ain't mean no harm. You know Nikki's a beautiful woman. And niggas gonna look at her. Let it go brother. It's my party" he said placing her arm around Big R's shoulder. "We here to have a good time; chill the fuck out man!" Big R acknowledged Q and apologized respectively. He'd lost control. Big R was always flamboyant and charismatic with his swag, exuberating the true essence of a gangster. He walked over and apologized to Derrick and excused himself from the party. "My bad, everybody have a good time" Big R's apology was fake. Deep down inside he resented the way Nikki and Derrick looked at each other and he'd been in the game long enough to know it was something going on between the two of them. And as far as he was concerned Derrick was now on his own personal shit list and only time and patience would allow him to seek his revenge. He would never forget this night. He felt like he was totally disrespected and embarrassed himself in the presence of fellow comrades.

How dare this chick be making eyes with another cat. She belonged to him.

Derrick's next six months proved to be as prosperous and rewarding as his past year and a half working for Q. He had no idea he would achieve so much so fast. He purchased a nice three bed room rancher in Woodlawn for him and his mom for $120,000.00 equipped with a wheel chair ramp and mini van to accommodate his moms physical limitations. Although her heart transplant was a success she still had some other medical diagnosis which gave her limited mobility. Derrick even hired a private duty nurse from a private duty agency called We Care Private Duty Services, which serviced the Baltimore region with skilled and qualified nurses to care for persons with medical ailments from post op surgery and rehabilitation to elderly patients with other personal health care needs. His moms private duty nurse named Ivy would visit her three days a week to make sure she was following her post-op hospital orders. Derricks mom had also suffered several mini strokes called T.I.A's prior to her heart transplant and was required to attend rehab three days a week in attempt for her to regain strength on the right side of her body. Fortunately for Derrick he was able to afford the coverage of a private duty nurse because sometimes he would be gone for weeks at a time.

CHAPTER 30

Prior to his initiation in to Q's organization January 1ˢᵗ 2001. Derrick was just a another solider in a hierarchy of elite hustlers getting money. But now he was officially a made-man. He was now a lieutenant with soldiers of his own that he supplied with cocaine that he would purchase wholesale from Q. Derrick was also put in charge of managing the stash houses. Unfortunately he was still on Big R's shit list. Big R was shrewd and calculative as Q and he was determined to get Derrick out the loop; by any means necessary. For the next following months Derrick continued to kick ass and was making major moves while protecting several million dollars for Q. The stash houses were filled with a couple hundred pounds of cocaine, heroin and millions of dollars in cash. The more Derrick excelled in Q's organization; The more adamant Big R was about getting him out. It was only a matter of time before he found out the truth about him and Nikki. This only added fuel to the fire. One evening when Big R was home ranting and raving about the night at the Christmas party. Nikki got fed up and told it all; heart and soul. She disclosed to Big R the intricate details about how good Derrick fucked her and how she wished she was with him. Big R was furious and his first response was to break her fucking neck. He swung at her face missing it by inches punching a huge whole in the wall. Had that punch connected, Nikki would've been seriously injured. Nikki ran for her life hiding in the huge four bedroom house as she'd done several times before when Big R was in a rage of fury. She was terrified.

How dare this $500.00 a night stripper from the block pull his gangsta card.

Who was she to say he was inadequate in bed when he provided and took care of her every need. It was he that took her off the block. It was he that paid all her bills. It was he that made sure she never wanted for nothing ; from Gucci to Fendi. $50,000.00 a month shopping sprees; from NYC to Paris. Nikki wore nothing but the best. She even had designer clothing, shoes, and purses she purchased on shopping trips to Italy.

Big R held much respect in the game and to him street credibility was everything. And he never allowed himself to be disrespected by anyone. As far as he was concerned Derrick was a dead man walking. It wasn't gonna be enough room for both of them in Q's organization and more importantly Nikki's heart. He refused to allow Derrick to play him out of position. In all honesty Big R felt much jealousy and animosity towards Derrick. Not only because he was coming up quick in the drug game establishing trust and admiration from Q, but also because the woman he loved and cherished showed something she'd never shown him. A genuine true love. Big R was fucked up that night off of cocaine and cognac, but he still remembered the look in Derrick and Nikki's eyes.

The chemistry between Nikki and Derrick was authentic . . . . The time was 4 o'clock. The July 6th, 88 degree sunny afternoon temperature was amplified by the agonizing sticky humidity which seemed to form a cloud of steamy fog over the Murdaland. The humidity always made the temperature feel 10 degrees hotter.

Days like this you needed to drink plenty of water and chill in the shade. A lot of kids would make freeze cups out of cool aid. This was the closest thing to a snowball in the hood. Derrick entered The Cherry Hill projects from down bottom passing through the shopping center enroute to his old Dojo in the recreation center on Spelman Rd.

Sunlight refracted off the wax that coated his red top less Nissan 300zx. He was greeted by some of his homies he grew up with as he passed through the Cherry Hill shopping center. "Derrick, what up nigga?" yelled Greg and David posted up on Greg's blue 300zx. getting money of their own. Derrick blew the horn. "What's up Yo!" he replied waving his arm out the top less 300zx. Greg's midnight blue turbo 300zx was just as fast as Derricks. Greg and David where in the game long before Derrick and operated independently. They had their own cliental and was making crazy loot of their own. Derrick was ahead of schedule for his rounds. Most of the stash houses were in Baltimore county. Derrick liked his new position as a lieutenant enforcing and protecting the drugs and monies kept in the stash houses much more better than kicking asses every other day on drug runs and collecting debts from idiots that fucked up the product or money.

During his rounds Derrick made sure four of the seven stash houses had no more than 20 kilos of pure fish scale cocaine and one million dollars in cash and the other three contained 20 kilos of pure heroin and a million dollars each. Most of the money was weighed in bundles on a scale. Only a select few people knew about the stash houses. Q, Big R, Derrick, and Q's chosen armed soldiers that guarded the stash houses 24 / 7. Q kept his stash houses on the low. Off the radar. Derrick was diligent and thorough in making his rounds. He was ahead of schedule after several hours of counting and weighing bundles of money and kilos of drugs. He had one house left. The last stash house was in Glen Burnie. Just 15mins from The Cherry Hill projects. After passing through the shopping center Derrick drove down Caver road to holla at a couple more homies. Everyone knew Derrick was getting money hustling because his demeanor had changed much since his early martial arts days. He was now flossin major chips and remained cool with other hustlers coming up in the drug game. Derrick left his homies parking his 300zx outside the rec center. Everyone in the hood knew it was his; so there was no need to put the tops in. Nobody was gonna fuck wit it.

It had been months since Derrick last visited Sensei-T. The scorching heat of the hot summer day had finally started to subside making the evening temperature much more desirable. Derrick stood in the doorway peering through the fog of steam from perspiration generated from the bodies of training martial artists under the instruction of Sensei-T. What a display of strength and dedication. Even after he was tragically gunned down and paralyzed he still instructed his Karate class. He and his top students filled the gymnasium. They ranked from beginner white belts to black belts; who were more advanced and skilled. Derrick marveled at Sensei-T's loyalty and dedication to his students and how he still had the courage and heart of a Lion with the respect of a fleet admiral of the United States Navy. Sensei-T was a master black belt who'd studied under the honorable martial arts master, Riley Hawkins. A former military veteran that had studied the arts in the orient and was so dedicated to Karate that he earned respect from martial artists nationwide. Even the honorably deceased martial artist Bruce Lee; A legend to the art of fighting participated in a tournament in the 1960'5 with the karate champion Riley Hawkins. Upon his discharge from activity military service Riley Hawkins became dedicated to teaching martial arts to urban kids in Baltimore with hopes of it instilling confidence, discipline, and a mindset of success in the inner city youth, however not all of the students used their martial training for positive purposes.

Sensei-T made his way from student to student via his wheelchair checking his students execution and technique. No Marty, from the hip. "Always throw your kicks from the hip. You'll generate more power" "Now Kick!" the young thirteen year old student followed Sensei-T's instruction attentively. The snap of his instep kick against the heavy bag geared from the hip proved to be more effective. The snapping impact of his kick echoed the gym. "Yes, very good" "Again!" exclaimed Sensei-T, as he rolled his wheelchair on to the another student who was sparring. "You're using too much energy over there Anthony. Just move your head and pivot your feet and counter, bob and weave.

You're expending too much energy running around" "Help him out Dino." "Show him how too allude punches and counter punch without expending energy" "yeah, yeah that's it" Derrick walked over to Sensei greeting him in formal Karate tradition, lowering his head eyes forward and bowing at the waist with his fist in palm. Sensei reciprocated the traditional martial arts greeting as a karate master would to his student. Sensei-T's left eyebrow raised slightly as he looked at Derrick with a look of disappointment and inquisitiveness. "So to whom do I owe this unexpected visit?" Derrick leaned forward embracing Sensei-T with a strong hug. The two of them looked like two lone surviving soldiers reuniting after a gruesome war. "So what's up Derrick. What brings you by the Dojo" "Let's hit that Chinese joint Sensei on Liberty rd. The Golden Dragon. You know that spot you use to take me and the other students after Karate tournaments back in the day" "It's my turn to treat you Sensei" Derrick exclaimed with a tone of sincere gratitude.

"Humm??" Sensei-T grunted. With a look of deep thought. "Ok, I need to talk to you about a few things anyway. But I won't have time to go to The Golden Dragon" "We can order take out from the shopping center here in Cherry Hill" "Ok Sensei-T. That's cool." Derrick answered, now with a tone of disappointment. He truly wanted to hang out with Sensei-T like he did back in the day. However much had changed and although Sensei-T loved Derrick like his own son he could not condone how Derrick utilized his pernicious martial arts skills for villainous purposes. "Dino, John-John, Byrd, and Jamie. run the class till I get back, I gotta head out for a few minutes" "Okay, no problem Sensei-T" The four senior black belts of the karate class said and began breaking the karate class down into groups of four as they had done many times before in Sensei-T's absence "Aight Derrick you stay cool bro" said Byrd. Derrick, Byrd, Dino, John-John, and Jamie were five of the most superb fighters of Sensei's students. The other students began bidding farewell to Derrick as well. Somewhere along the line Derrick had chosen a path of destruction and he wasn't the first or the last of martial art fighters to use their elite fighting skills for the purposes of corruption. Derrick held the door for Sensei-T as he wheeled his chair out of the gymnasium. The transfer from wheelchair to Derrick's 300zx was relatively easy since he had the T-tops out. As soon as Derrick opened the car door, Sensei shifted his weight to his arms and propelled himself into the black leathered covered seat effortlessly. At least it appeared that way from anyone who observed.

Although he was paralyzed from the waist down from the gun shot wounds he sustained the day of the ATM robbery he still maintained a level of supreme martial arts skills and stupendous physical ability. Derrick popped the hatch placing Sensei-T's folded wheel chair in the back of the 300zx and hopped in the drivers seat starting the ignition.

"She sounds good!" marveled Sensei-T. "What you got 250, 300 horse power under the Hood?" "300 boasted Derrick shifting his baby 300zx into 2nd gear as he spun a U turn on Spelman Rd. shifting into 3rd gear slightly spinning wheels. "Oh yeah" marveled Sensei she can run!" Derrick was parked in front of the Chinese joint in the shopping center in a matter of seconds. "What can I get you Sensei-T you're usual chicken and vegetables?"

"Yeah, sounds good Derrick. You've got a good memory" "I forgot the traditional name for it Sensei" Derrick said with a look of inquisition. "Moo goo ga pan" answered Sensei-T with his charismatic smile. "oh yeah that's right" laughed Derrick entering the store. "Yo Derrick whut up kid. How you been man. Long time long see" said Wayne. Along time friend of Derrick he grew up with back in the day. "I like dat 300zx son. That joint is tight" "Hey Wayne what's up fam. that Monte Carlo SS you got ain't to be played wit either" "Yeah she can do a little sumpin, sumpin" smiled Wayne exiting the store. "Aight Derrick you stay cool man. Peace" "Aight Wayne, peace" replied Derrick ordering the Chinese food.

Derrick returned to the car while he and Sensei waited for their order. He could tell by Sensei-T's facial expression something was wrong. "So Derrick, looks like life's treating you pretty good. Your mom was able to get her heart operation. I heard you, brought you and her a new home out in Woodlawn county, Plus you got a brand new candy apple turbo 300zx. You doin good for yourself huh?" "I'm doin ok." shrugged Derrick.

He knew by Sensei's tone and expression where he was goin with his accolades and sarcastic comments. However Derrick knew Sensei-T's comments were not derived from jealousy, but from genuine concern. Derrick was like his son and he would never want nothing but the best for him, provided the odds of repercussion were favorable for the path of making money he'd chosen. Sensei had lost many a pupil over the years; skilled martial arts students who decided they wanted to be hustlers. "How long do you think its gonna last son?" "Sooner or later it will catch up with you. Karma is real. And you will (reap what you sow) "If you needed extra cash you could always fight more professional fights. We all know you got robbed you're 1st fight. Everybody knows you won that fight Derrick" Derrick responded with a tone of fearlessness. "I'll find my own way Sensei. I gotta be my own man; come what may. You always taught us to be responsible for our actions and believe in ourselves. I'm doing what I have to do to survive"

Sensei-T's eyebrows raised completely, he was dumbfounded. "That's bullshit Derrick! you're taking the easy way out. And you know it. You may as well have sold your soul to the devil. Q is a wicked man. Do you know how many of my students he's tried to recruit over the years. He knows we are the best when it comes to killing a motherfucker and the most disciplined when it comes to loyalty and dependability. He's using you"

"Q's the devil's advocate and now you've become one of his primary disciples. How many men have you killed or disabled for him already? "Derrick could not deny his affiliation with Q, nor could he deny his numerous encounters with death in which he'd slain many hustler's and gangsters that tried to bring shit to the drug game. It was kill or be killed. The evening hour was closing fast, it was almost 9pm and Derrick still had one last stash house to check in Glen Burnie. Derrick was beginning to feel shame and guilt as he drove Sensei back to the rec center. He turned up the stereo in the 300zx to transform the morbid sound of silence to a more cheerful airspace. DJ Boobie was mixing it up on V-103 airwaves with the club jams. Derrick swerved the corner in his 300zx on Spelman Rd. parking in front of the rec center. He popped the hatch removing Sensei-T's wheelchair. Before he could open the door Sensei was halfway off the passenger seat. At that moment he leaped in his wheelchair as effortlessly as he'd gotten out of it.

Derrick went to shake Sensei's hand, but was thrown slightly off balance as he pulled him close to him. "Derrick I love you like a son, but your association with crime misrepresents what Riley Hawkins has taught me and what I have taught you. Karate is a disciplined art that was created with the purpose of protecting and sustaining life; not destroying it for selfish gain." Derrick and Sensei-T where shoulder to shoulder. Derrick placed his hand on the wheelchair to maintain his balance. "Don't allow your foolish actions to cause you to self destruct. No action; just or unjust goes unanswered."

"Remember the saying, "For every action there is an equal and opposite reaction"

Derrick could feel the concern and sincerity in Sensei-T's voice and held nothing but the utmost respect for him. Derrick released his hand clasp and closed the hatch of his 300zx. He could anticipate what was gonna be said next and he was right. Sensei-T would tell him to stay away from his Dojo. "You've placed many lives in danger Derrick and don't even know it. Needless to mention the reputation of our Dojo. Don't you know our younger students see you older guys as role models. They practically worship the ground you and the other senior black belts walk on. We can't subject any of them to your drug dealing life style. You're a negative influence Derrick and can no longer come around my Dojo. You could have them getting mixed up in shit they have no idea of.

Look at those mother fuckers over there in the black Nissan Pathfinder, they followed us to the shopping center. Did you notice?" "Yeah I saw them fools" Derrick said nonchalantly. Derrick wasn't certain but it looked like two of Big R's crew.

"What the hell are they following me for?" Derrick thought to himself. Something didn't feel right. "Handle your business son. Just don't bring that shit around here anymore. Think about what I said Derrick and most all don't forget where the hell you came from" Sensei-T spun himself around in his wheelchair turning his back to Derrick, who felt like he was being exiled. And in all actuality he was. Sensei-T wanted Derrick to have no affiliation, association or interaction with the Dojo or any of the students as long as he was affiliated with the drug game. Derrick jumped in his 300zx revving the engine never looking back. The burnt smell of his Pirelli sport tires on gold BBS rims fumed as they spun on the street covered black asphalt. "Damn where dat nigga goin ?" asked Ron, Starting the engine of the black Nissan Pathfinder, "Shit I don't Yo, but follow his ass. You know Big R said keep our eyes on his every move" Derrick gunned his 300zx down Spelman Rd. and then sped down the bottom of Round Rd. doin about 60mph. He blew his horn at some of his homies posted up down the bottom getting money. Damn son ain't dat that kid Derrick. Shorty pushin dat 300zx smiled Keith. "I gotta black one like that" Derrick made his way to Hanover street bridge going toward Brooklyn Homes and slowed down as he passed the Stock Market Bar. Ron and Grimy had just reached the bottom of Round Rd. "Who dezz niggas?" yelled Keith to his four man team. Revealing everything from 9mm's to Tech-9's. "Oh shit keep goin"

Yelled Grimy, "These niggas must think we stick up boys trying to rob them"

"Man you know these Cherry Hill niggaz crazy, get us the fuck outta here before they kill our ass!!!" "Shut up you pussy ass nigga!" responded Ron. Pop-pop . . . pop. pop rang off gun shots from the bottom of the hill as Ron and Grimy proceeded towards Hanover street bridge. "Yo I'm bout ready to go back and blast them fools." said Grimy removing a 38. caliber revolver from his pant belt. "Nigga put dat shit up fo yo ass shoot yourself or me wit dat bitch. If you was gonna shoot, you would've been pulled dat joint out back on the strip" Grimy slid his 38. Revolver back between his pant belt.

He was insulted that Ron pulled his bitch card. "Fuck you Ron! you non driving motherfucker. You need to find out which way that nigga went!" Grimy said nervously. "If we lose dat nigga Big R gonna fuck both our asses up. Which way dat nigga go man?" speak for yourself. Laughed Ron. "You scary ass Nigga! Ha, ha . . ."

CHAPTER 31

Derrick was able to allude Ron and Grimy's tail successfully and he also managed to do so without getting a ticket from local authorities. Especially on Gov. Ritchie Highway. Which stayed busy with county officers ready to pull over traffic violators.

This particular stash house, Derrick always saved for last. Not only was it close to his old Dojo in Cherry Hill it was also close to a fine, older sophisticated lady named Sharon he would kick it with who resided Glen Burnie. Sharon was a fine Venessa Williams looking chick. Totally independent and self-sufficient. The kinda chick that held her own. The average Joe could never hold her interest. She only fucked with real go getters. And even though Derrick was ten years younger than her he was definitely a go-getter.

Sharon was in her late thirties but looked like she was in her early twenties; her body was to die for. At 5'5" her large 38DD succulent breast where more than an eye catcher; they demanded attention from the most devoted man. Her hips curved incredibly, complimenting her perfect rounded ass. Her face was as beautiful as a piece of art work by Michael Angelo. Her eyes sparkled like flawless diamonds and her beautiful smile could cheer the most darkened and despaired of hearts. However, to Derrick the most sacred attribute Sharon possessed was her honesty. She was never one to bite her tongue and always spoke what was on her mind. Derrick had planned to take Sharon to Mo's Sea Food across from the Inner Harbor after checking Q's last stash house, but little did he know it would literally be his last round. Big R's scandalous plan was in full effect and Derrick was about to be a SCAPEGOAT . . . .

CHAPTER 32

Derrick arrived in front of the stash house at 9:55p.m. His usual arrival time was between 9:30p.m. and 10'O clock. He was on schedule and everything appeared to be on point. The only thing that aroused his suspension was a dark blue mini van parked a few houses down on the opposite side of the street. In clinical terms Derrick would have been evaluated as a individual with a photo graphic memory, however in street terms he would be defined as a nigga wit good survival instincts. The two things that aroused Derricks suspicion was one, the dark blue mini van parked on an angle indicating it was positioned to make a quick exit; and second the extreme window tint was out of place compared to the other vehicles usually parked on that particular street.

Most of the block consisted of middle class white and black residents that worked. And their vehicles ranged from 1979 Chevy Nova's to 1990 Chevy Camaro's and Ford Pick-ups. Derricks red turbo 300zx was one of the fastest and finest on the block and everyone thought he was the son of a rich real estate investor. Little did they know Derrick was a enforcer and drug runner for an elaborate organized crime family lead by Q. Q's stash houses were always kept in low, middle, and upper class neighborhoods to alleviate suspicion.

Derrick walked casually up to the front door of the stash house as he always did; but tonight he felt something was up. He continued to glance back momentarily at the dark blue minivan in case someone tried to bring him a move. Derrick was about to place his key in the door, but noticed the front door was slightly ajar. "Fuck this!" he said to himself as he turned to walk off the porch. "This shit don't feel right" at that moment the sound of a 44. magnum hammer cocking a few inches from the back of his head filled him with an instant rage. He knew something was going down. Two armed ski masked gunmen instructed Derrick to walk slowly back into the stash house making sure to keep a safe distance from his lightening quick feet and hands. Once inside the masked gunmen made sure to speak loudly. "Hey Derrick, what's up boss" Yeah man bout time you got here" stated the other gunmen. Derrick was staring into the gun barrels of two ruthless killers. He wasn't close enough to disarm them and knew he had no choice but to play along with their deceitful scheme. The gunmen continued their charade talking boastfully as if Derrick was the mastermind of the heist. "We got the loot and drugs like you told us boss, its back in the kitchen"

"You mother fuckers are so full of shit!" Derrick thought to himself.

He proceeded to walk back towards the kitchen as instructed knowing if he made one false move he would be shot dead. Passing through the living room he noticed the two men that usually guarded the stash house were tied with their arms behind their back in chairs; duct tape covered their mouth's and blindfolds covered their eyes. "That son of a bitch!!" Derrick mumbled angrily. He knew for sure he'd been set up and was almost certain who the culprit was. Who else would go to such extremes to humiliate him. If someone wanted him dead their goons could've killed him on the spot and made it look like a robbery. But no, this had more to do with assassination of character opposed to the assassination of his life. Big R knew the way to really hurt Derrick was not a quick death, but a slow humiliating one. He wanted Derrick to suffer and feel the humiliation he did. And Big R was a master at seeking vengeance . . . .

As Derrick entered the kitchen a bright blue, spectrum of light was all he remembered as the butt of a shot-gun thrashed against the back of his occipital lope rendering him unconscious. Big R's ski-masked gunmen worked diligently carrying out his diabolical plan. They removed his car keys from his left pant pocket and placed a blind folded over his eyes made of a black bandana. "This nigga ain't getting his hands loose from this" stated one of the ski-masked gunmen as he tied Derrick hands behind his back.

"If he do dat's your ass" joked another one of the gunmen. "You know dat niggas hands and feet is deadly ass shit. You might want to tie his feet together, while you bull shittin worrying bout his hands. He fuck around and kick the shit out you!"

"Ain't nobody scared of his fucking feet." proclaimed the gunmen. "Yeah ok, if he fuck you up Big R gonna be dealing wit your ass" "Fuck it" stated the gunmen. Make sure dat nigga feet tied man" he knew if Derrick was to get away he'd have to answer to Big R. and that could mean losing his life. "Ok tell them to pull around the back alley so we can put his ass in the minivan" two of the gunmen removed their ski mask and exited the rear of the stash house carrying Derrick wrapped up in an old rug to camouflage his appearance just in case any neighbors where watching. After loading Derrick's unconscious body into the mini-van. One of the gunmen returned inside the stash house. He donned his ski masked and walked into the room with the guards tied up in the chairs. POP . . . . POP . . . . POP . . . rang off his 45. caliber handgun as the mussel flashed red with smoke. Blood spattered across the room as one of the two stash house guards bodies slummed over limp in his chair. Shattered skull fragments and white and gray brain matter ran down his shoulders. The other guard was spared to tell the tale.

As far as he knew from what was heard Derrick was the culprit of the stash house heist and execution of the guard. The gunman threw the gun in one the two duffle bags filled with money. The one with the murder weapon would go in Derricks car.

The gunman flung his gray Russell sweat hood over his head and slid the two duffle bag strap's over his shoulders as he exited the stash house en-route to Derrick's 300zx. He popped the hatch throwing the duffle bags with the gun and money in the back. He then drove off in candy apple red 300zx to meet up with the rest of the ski-masked crew at Big R's abandoned warehouse.

CHAPTER 33

Derrick awoke to a bucket of water being thrown in his face. His feet had been cut loose but his hands were still tied behind his back. One of the four ski-masked goons walked over snatching off Derricks blindfold. "Ok motherfucker, are you ready for the ass whipping of your life" before Derrick could blink a fist smashed him in the face, busting his lip. Derrick rolled in the direction of the punch on his right side and managed to sit up on his left knee.

A gush of air passed Derrick's head by inches as one of the other ski-masked goons attempted to bang him in the face. Before he could snap his punch back, Derrick let out a loud "Ki-YA!!" sound which came from a immanent place deep from within his core self. A inner power which only a trained martial artist could summon. Derrick leaped in the air smashing two of his assailants ribs with his left knee. "Awe . . . . damn!" scrabbled the other three reaching for what ever they could get their hands on. They were instructed by Big R to beat Derrick within inches of his life, but not to kill him.

But Derrick was no chump and it wasn't gonna be as easy as they thought. One of the gunman picked up a two foot pole that resembled a fence post he attempted to swing at Derrick's head only to be greeted by a side kick smashing into the right side of his face snapping his jaw bone, which sounded like a crab shell being smashed by a mallet.

"Ahhh!!!" cried the gunmen, his face disfigured falling to the ground. "Man we gonna have to shoot this nigga" yelled one of the other gunmen. At that moment he grabbed a fire extinguisher spraying it in Derricks face blinding him momentarily.

Derrick tried desperately to regain his bearing only to feel a 4x4 smashing into the side of his face.

The other gunman picked up the pole and began hitting him in his legs breaking them in several places. The two gunmen began beating Derrick relentlessly until he lost consciousness. Derrick was left in the abandoned warehouse with a fractured jaw, three broken ribs, and two fractured legs. The total take from the stash house was 1 million dollars in cash. Two duffle bags contained $500,000.00 each. One of the bags of money containing the murder weapon used to execute the stash house guard would be left in the hatch of Derricks 300zx. The other $500,000.00 bag of money would be later delivered to Big R by his goons at his elaborate house in Owings Mills. Derrick would definitely look like the perpetrator. And Big R was gonna make sure of it. He made sure to stay in Q's presence the whole day to ensure he had an air tight alibi for himself. Most of the day he hung out with Q at the pool sipping mixed drinks and checking out the beautiful selection of women at his estate. Big R had received a coded text on his beeper indicating his goons had completed their mission. The coded text was 0000. Which was to indicate the stash house was left with no money. And that Derrick was at the abandoned warehouse.

Once Big R got his beep. He was really ready to assassinate Derricks character. The whole day he had been bringing up the issue of trust and how there could be some weak links in his organization. However Big R's primary motive was to discourage Q from trusting Derrick and now his plan was in full effect. Time and a few phone calls would take care of the rest making this evenings heist all the more believable for Derrick to have performed.

CHAPTER 34

Big R arrived home a little after midnight. He was already fucked up from the mixed drinks at Q's and was already for a toast with his goons. Except for the two that had been hospitalized at Harbor hospital; one with three fractured ribs and the other with his mouth wired shut from a broken jaw. Derrick was a deadly martial artist even with both hands tied behind his back. "Here's too you two mother fucker's for bringing me my loot and not letting Lil Bruce Leroy whip yall ass like dem other two weak ass niggas laying up in the hospital" Big R and his goons toasted with glasses of Rose Moet.

They all laughed as he continued to boast and brag about how he set Derrick up to look like he robbed the stash house. "That little karate kid is done. You see that's how you handle cocky bastards like that. You let them defeat themselves. Little nigga tried to show me up to Q at the damn Christmas party. Now we'll see who gets the last laugh.

Q is gonna be done wit dat kid. He's as good as dead "Big R's speech was slurred and it was obvious he'd had too much to drink. He was totally oblivious; talking a little too much for his own good. He failed to realize Nikki was sitting at the top of the stairs listening to his boastful ego going on and on about how great he was as usual when he'd had too much to drink or snort. "Let's see him kick his way outta The Spot" "The Spot?" Nikki thought to herself. Kick his way out? Embarrassed at the Christmas party?

Nikki was able to figure out the rest, as to who Big R's victim was without him saying another word. She knew he was talking about Derrick. "Oh my God!" she thought to her self as her heartbeat began to race as if it where about to pound out of her chest. "What is The Spot' I've heard this before" "The Spot; The Spot" she repeated to herself. "oh shit it's the abandoned warehouse he's always bragging about where he kills people that double crossed him" Nikki was on point and never thought that after months of listening to Big R boast and brag that it would ever really mattered; until today.

At that moment the telephone rang. "Yeah?" Big R answered in his usual nonchalant tone. He already knew who was calling. It was Q about the heist and murder at the stash house; However Big R continued to play dumb as if he had know idea what Q was talking about. "What man, get the hell outta here" Big R was a master at bullshitting and today he won the bullshit award. "Any idea who could've hit it man?"

"You know Q I hate to say it, but there's something about your boy Derrick I never trusted. He got that hustlers greed in his eyes man. I never felt comfortable around that kid" "Shit!" responded Q. on the other end of the phone. I been paging him for the past two hours and he hasn't responded. That's not like Derrick, he always called back within a matter of minutes when I paged him. We gotta have a meeting. I want you at my place tomorrow morning. We gonna get to the bottom of this shit!!" CLICK . . . Big R stood there momentarily listening to the dial tone. He could tell Q was furious and that's just how he wanted him to be. "Ha, ha, ha . . . ." laughed Big R placing the phone on the receiver. He stumbled over to his favorite black leather chair where he collapsed like a puppet whose strings had been released by his puppeteer.

This wasn't the first time his goons saw him pass out after an over consumption of alcohol or drugs. They placed the duffle bag containing the $500,000.00 beside the leather easy chair he collapsed in. "We out boss, hey Boss we out" they said exiting his house. Big R was motionless, his brain buoyant, floating in a pool alcohol and cranial fluid. His neural synopsis was rendered to a standstill as if he were in a coma of some sort or anesthetized. Nikki slipped on her pink Nike sweat suit and a pair of Nike sneakers preparing to get the hell out of there. She couldn't stand to be in Big R's presence another minute. It took every ounce of restraint she could muster to keep from smashing him over the head with a flower vase that sat on a table just a few feet away from the black recliner he passed out in. "Oh I want too so bad!" she mumbled to her self as she walked by him placing her hands firmly around the crystal flower vase. She began to lift it slowly above her head in position to slam down on his head. She slid her foot to the side to widen to her stance when it bumped the duffle bag full of money sitting on the floor beside Big R. She sat the vase back on the table and leaned over to open the duffle bag on the floor. She felt a chill in her body that made her slightly shiver. She had been around hundreds of thousands of dollars before, but never half a million of them at one time; In so many denominations.

Nikki zipped the duffle bag back up and slid it across the floor. She knew her leaving him and taking his money would be worst than killing him. And she wanted him to suffer the pain he'd inflicted on her over the years with his drunken stupors and abuse.

And most of all she wanted him to suffer for the hurt he'd caused the only man she'd ever truly grown to love and respect. The bond between Derrick and Nikki was one founded on honesty and trust. It was only circumstances that pulled them apart, but now it was fate that would bring them together. Nikki slid the duffle bag back into the kitchen and out into the garage. Parked side by side was a white Lexus LS 400 and a white 560SEL Mercedes Benz. Both top of the line of course. Nikki grabbed the keys to the 560 SEL popping the trunk. It took every ounce of strength she had to lift the duffle bag of money into the trunk of the Benz but she did it. Tears streamed down her face as her heart pounded with anticipation. Her biggest concern now was if Derrick would still be alive.

It was amazing how certain life events could bring someone to a mind state of self-awareness and steadfast realization. Nikki had no idea she had such strong emotional ties to Derrick, at least not until now.

She knew she cared about him, but at this point felt she would do anything for him; even if it meant leaving her comfort zone at Big R's estate with his lavish life style which accommodated her on every level in a material sense; however he failed to satisfy her needs emotionally. Nikki was always capable of making her own money, but allowed herself to be swept into Big R's world of being her sole provider. Nikki's foot pressed firmly on the accelerator of the white 560 SEL as she swerved in and out of traffic and onto 695 south to exit 11B. Her eyes were bloodshot red and almost blinded with streams of tears flooding her face running down her cheeks.

The next few minutes Nikki would arrive to the abandoned warehouse in Fairfield. An industrial park community on Chesapeake Ave. that contained many business's. She obtained the exact address from one of Big R's property bills of sales kept in their basement home office before she left.

She always remembered him referring to the Fairfield property as the Spot. Nikki pulled into the industrial park community driving down to Big R's warehouse which looked unused compared to many of the other buildings in the area. She pulled in front of the building shifting the transmission of the 560SEL into park. Her heart pumped with adrenaline as she removed a flashlight from the trunk of the car and proceeded to find entrée to the building. The flashlight shinned bright beneath the dim moonlit sky.

Nikki's heart rate continued to accelerate to over a hundred beats per minute as her imagination ran wild with thoughts of how she would find Derrick in the warehouse.

She proceeded to walk with caution shinning the flashlight slowly side to side. The huge front sliding door of the warehouse was slightly ajar. Nikki pushed the sliding door with all her might until it opened completely allowing the moon lit sky and street lights to shine inside almost illuminating the inside of the building. Shallow breath sounds could be heard from the rear of the building. "Derrick, Derrick!" Nikki said desperately calling his name. "Derrick is that you?" Nikki lifted the flashlight in the direction of the breath sounds and almost collapsed. Derrick was a bloodied mess. She would've thought he was dead had she not heard his shallow breath sounds. Derrick attempted to raise up off the floor only to gasp a breath from his agonizing pain. "Damn it!!" he cursed collapsing back to the floor. "Oh baby!" Nikki said running to his side. "What did those bastards do to you" no doubt Derrick was experiencing excruciating pain.

Nikki attempted to assist him only to inflict more pain. "Ah shit!" Derrick yelled.

"I'm sorry Derrick" Nikki said sorrowfully. Pain or no pain Derrick knew he had to get the hell outta that warehouse. It would be only a matter of seconds, minutes, or hours before Big R and his goons returned to finish up the job. Being a trained martial artist Derrick would attempt to test the epitome of his elite martial arts skills of mind over matter. This was truly a test of his life; in retrospect for his life. Derrick concentrated immensely in attempt to block out all the death wrenching pain he was experiencing at the present moment.

It felt like someone was slicing open his flesh with a knife each time he attempted to stand. He had no choice but to slide himself across the floor, dragging his broken leg and grasping the left side of his rib cage containing two broken ribs. Nikki reached down pulling him with every bit of strength she could phantom, while holding onto the flashlight. "Come on Derrick, we gotta get the fuck outta here!" Nikki dropped the flashlight pulling Derrick through the warehouses sliding door. "Wait here baby" she said running over to the idling Mercedes pulling it up next to Derrick. Beads of sweat formed his forehead and proceeded to flow profusely from his pores. His white Tee was now completely saturated with blood and perspiration. Derrick looked like he was on deaths door and the Grim Reaper was about to carry his ass home to eternity . . . .

Derrick felt himself slipping to a point of unconsciousness, but refused to allow himself to give up. He could feel the depths of his desire to sleep leading to an eternal death bed.

"NO!!" he exclaimed fighting his pain reaching over for the opened passenger side door handle. Nikki attempted to hold his shoulders from behind ready to lift Derrick up onto the car seat. With one hand draped over the edge of the car seat and the other gripped tightly on the door handle he proceeded to lift. Nikki stood closely behind him with her hands under his arm pits. "Ok Nikki, on three baby" "One, two, three" Derricks eyes were closed and his mind state transcended to levels of intense concentration.

All his focus was on his internal strength locked into his Ki. An ancient Asian martial arts term used to define ones depth of internal power that coincided with the universe. A man's Ki, allowed him to utilize his internal power to the utmost, demonstrating and performing amazing feats of strength and abilities which seemed extraordinary to the common man. The Ki is located three inches below the naval of every human being, according to ancient Asian culture. And although he was an African American with a blend of Indian and Irish; At this moment his core essence emanated back to the origins of a Japanese Samurai Warrior. Even the manner of his persona as hired protection to those with power and money seemed to stem back to the theory of the ancient "Samurai" And "Ronin" Which was grounded in the concepts of Bushido; THE WAY OF THE WARRIOR. The honorable concept of Bushido is freedom from fear of death. Samurai warriors of ancient Japan were legally entitled to use their martial arts skills to mame or kill anyone who failed to honor them properly.

To dishonor a Samurai was the ultimate form of insult. Much like hired gunslingers of the Western world like Doc holiday and Wild Bill; however eastern Japanese culture had its own hired hands by way of the Samurai armed with a lethal 36" long blade, that was crafted to perfection. A one of a kind sword designed for the one of a kind warrior that handled the blade.

The spirit of the Bushido warrior ran deep, and the concepts of internal strength even deeper. This is what allowed Sensei-T, Derrick, Byrd, Dino, John-John, and many other trained martial arts fighters to demonstrate extraordinary feats of strength and power.

Bruce Lee was another prime example of an incredible martial artist that mastered the art of fighting; which made him and his son Brandon Lee exceptional fighters.

For they too were fearless warriors. At this point in Derricks life he realized he had to go back to the true essence of who he was. What Sensei-T told him was true. Derrick had experienced his moment of truth . . . .

CHAPTER 35

Watching Derrick exhibit the strength he did and pain he endured made her realize just how strong he was and a stern believer of the fact he was a true warrior. Which made her feelings for him even that more intense; she catered to his strength. Nikki closed the passenger side door and pulled away from The Spot knowing she'd made the right decision. All she was concerned with at this point was saving her man. Who was fighting desperately for his life. Being a certified nurse Nikki performed a quick assessment on Derrick and knew he needed care in a health care facility, but it was too risky. The hospital would be the first place Big R and his goons would look.

The only place Nikki knew Derrick would be safe was at her parents estate in Monkton.

Nikki hit the beltway taking 695 N. As much as she dreaded going home she had no choice. There was no-one else she trusted . . . . Nikki pulled the 560SEL around to the back of her parents estate and parked in what was now the guest house. It use to be Nikki's little domain before she left home to be on her own. The two bedroom guest house was modest, but had many updated amenities; That included a shower, washer, dryer, and remodeled kitchen. A lot had changed since Nikki had left. The entire estate sat on 2.5 acres of land. Due to several smart investments her dad had made with an investment firm called, Alex Brown and Sons, Dr. Jones and his wife were able to retire early and travel the world and also provide for their children's education. Nikki being so rebellious natured refused to allow them to do anything for her. Little did she know several years later she would need them more now than she would've ever imagined.

Before Nikki could shut off the engine her dad was enroute to the guest house.

There wasn't too much that went down on his estate he wasn't aware of.

Once an old investment banker friend named Ben told him. "Jim, If you really know what's goin on, you don't have to know what's goin on to know what's goin on" "Dad!"

Nikki said startled as her father approached the idling Mercedes.

She was so preoccupied with how Derrick was doing she didn't see him approach the car.

"Hey there my Lil Nik-Nik" so what do your mom and I owe for this surprise visit?"

At that moment he saw the blood dripping from Derricks swollen face as he sat quietly trying to conceal his excruciating pain in the passenger seat of the car. "Oh my God Nikki is he ok, we need to get him to a hospital ASAP" "Dad No, please. No hospitals and no police" a look of confusion and discontent formed Dr. Jones face. Immediately he knew they were on the run and initially he thought it was from the law. "What the hell is goin on Nichole, who are you on the run from?" Nikki knew for certain her father was concerned; it had been years since he'd addressed her by her government name.

"It's a long story dad" "Yes it always is, but right now this young man needs medical attention. Let's get him into the guest house" Nikki and her dad helped Derrick into the guesthouse and onto the living room sofa. "I'll be back, I'm gonna get my medical bag. Make sure this young man stays awake. Don't let him fall asleep. Looks like he's experienced tremendous head trauma" "Ok" Nikki said seating herself next to Derrick.

"Thanks dad, oh and do we have to tell mom?" Dr. Jones turned to Nikki with a sarcastic grin. "Are you kidding, she's probably already on her way down here" at that very moment her mom entered the guest house. "Jesus Christ, what's going on here, who's this young man. Nikki are you alright?"

"It's ok sweetie, he's a friend of Nichole's. He was in a lil accident"

"Accident my ass! With who Mike Tyson?" Nikki's mom said aloud. "Bullshit!!!" she knew it was more to this story then met the eye. "Come with me dear I'm gonna get my medical bag from the house," Dr. Jones took his wife by the hand exiting the guest house looking back momentarily at Nikki. "Thanks dad," she said with a silent sincerity so her mom didn't hear. Her dad nodded his head acknowledging her thanks making his way out the door. "Make sure he stays awake Nikki!" he yelled back once more. The next day her father called in a favor to one of his colleagues for an order of antibiotics to make sure Derrick wouldn't encounter any type of infection. There wasn't much Dr. Jones hadn't seen being he was a retired Ortho surgeon with also many years of internal medicine experience. After a few local anesthetics, sutures, bone stabilizations, and antibiotic's Derrick was set. The rest depended on time and the healing of Derricks wounds. Pain management wasn't much of a factor. Dr. Jones was amazed at Derricks pain tolerance level. Derrick refused any further pain meds after the first few days of recovery. His wounds healed nicely over the course of the next few weeks.

However; he wasn't the only one healing. So was Nikki and her distant ailing relationship with her mom and dad. For years they hadn't spoken and it was so ironic that such a life threatening encounter would bring them back together. As far as they were concerned they were happy to see their daughter alive and breathing under any circumstances. Growing up Nikki was rebellious but was never a problem child.

Chapter 36

6 months had passed and Derrick was almost fully recovered. Gradually he resumed his martial arts training in a quiet isolated wooded area on Nikki's families estate. For hours he would perform katas and meditate. He also began using deep concentration and lethal karate skills breaking old cement blocks and boards with his hands and feet.

Derrick found the center blocks and boards in the back of the guest house that were left over after renovations. Early one morning while performing katas Dr. Jones approached Derrick after about 20 minutes of observation. Derrick demonstrated lightening quick speed. "You've got great technique Derrick" he said walking over to him." How long have you been studying karate?" "Since I was about ten years old sir" Derrick said respectfully. "You know Derrick, my wife and I could never thank you enough for bringing our little girl back to us. We were beginning to think we would never see here again. We renovated the guest house though for her just in case she ever wanted to come back home. Although, I must say the circumstances were quite unusual"

Derrick walked over to Dr. Jones extending his hand. "Excuse me sir but with all due respect I should be thanking you for saving my life"

"No problem son. You're very strong. I don't know too many men who could have sustained the injuries you did and recover so quickly. I don't know what brought you and my daughter together or what you guys encountered out there and to be honest I really don't want to know as long as you got it all under control. What I do know is I have not seen her this happy in years and she seems to love you dearly. You and Nikki are welcome to stay here as long as you like. Just be wise and stay away from whatever it was that almost cost you your life. It's not worth it" Derrick nodded in acknowledgement. He appreciated Dr. Jone's honesty. His concern was genuine and he had every intention of he and Nikki starting a new life together, but soon all of his earnest intentions of starting a new life would change. The horrific events that would take place over the next couple of weeks would push Derrick over the edge; sending him on a relentless endeavor to kill Q and Big R; who would go to extreme measures to bring him out of hiding. Call it foresight, intuition, or mere luck. But just weeks prior to Derrick's run in with Big R's goons at The Spot he'd made arrangements with a trustee to make all payments to his moms private duty agency. He knew although he was capable of taking care of her business affairs himself; even he could get it. No one was exempt from death. Especially in his line of business. Derrick's mom meant the world to him and there was nothing he wouldn't do to assure her wellbeing.

The top story of news headlines featured an unbelievable story that made stomachs turn and eyes water nationwide. How could anyone be so evil, cruel, and sinister.

"Tonight's top story brings much sadness. And contains adult content. It is advised if you have children viewing the news to change the channel or have them leave the room"

"Woman's body found by private duty nurse naked, strangled, and chest cavity cut open with a blooded chain saw found left at the crime scene. At the present moment there are no motives or suspects . . . more news to come at eleven" . . . .

One month after Derrick and Nikki had gone into hiding Big R convinced Q it was Derrick that orchestrated the heist of the stash houses 6 months ago. And Q was not a man you want seeking vengeance on you. His was known to be ruthless with his tactics and the blood that was sacrificed upon initiation into his criminal empire was held to a high pedigree; as that of a priest being sworn into the inner sanctorum of priest hood.

Although Q's initiation into his criminal organization was very theatrical it was not based upon any religious beliefs or cult. It was based upon a code of the streets in which he placed his high moral value of sacrifice and honor. The initiation of some organizations required the taking of a life or getting ones ass beat to be affiliated. However Q requested a 5ml of blood extracted in a 15cc syringe, Which was ejected onto a section of ground of his 60 acre estate.

This blood was to symbolize life & death; anyone that betrayed his code would have to pay the ultimate price with his life. However Derrick's situation created a totally different scenario and since Q couldn't find Derrick. He felt entitled to take back the heart he'd had placed into Derrick's moms body. As far as Q was concerned Derrick stole from him so he was taking back the heart he'd purchased for his mom's transplant. It wasn't so much about the money as it was about the principle. Q felt entitled, regardless of morality or conscience which told him his orders to have Derrick's heart removed by his goons was extreme. But, Q felt betrayed and violated. So Derricks mom would have to pay the ultimate price. Q wanted her dead and Big R was thrilled at the fact Derrick was no longer a threat to him. Derrick was now an enemy to Q which meant Big R remained his number one go to guy in the criminal empire. Q also ordered the execution of Derrick's two soldiers, as far as he knew they could've been in on the heist also. Q trusted no-one.

Chapter 37

Derrick had just finished his morning workout which was now more intense since he was now back to his optimum training level. After running for an hour he would perform strength training in Dr. Jones personal gym in the basement. That contained all state of the art equipment. Derrick trained to the peak of his martial arts skill level. He was one lethal fighting machine capable of dislocating a cervical vertebra with the snap of an instep kick to the back of an assailants head. His speed, accuracy, and power increased to an optimum level proficiency. Derrick could kill a man with his bare hands in seconds.

He increased his knowledge of the human body with additional studies of anatomy and Physiology. He applied them to his martial arts knowledge of breaking bones and pressure points, many of which were illustrated on diagrams in Dr. Jones medical books that contained in depth photos and illustrations which provided him with additional knowledge of striking points that aided him in killing and laming his adversaries more quickly. Derrick was drenched with sweat as he proceeded towards the house. He'd just completed his two hour workout for the day. Something was different about today he thought to himself entering the kitchen door which provided an unbelievable view to the Jones estate. Especially Mrs. Jones personal garden which was similar to that of creative gardening from Ladew Gardens in Monkton MD; which was absolutely breath taking.

However, Mrs. Jones garden was much smaller, yet contained many of the same exotic flowers and awesome landscaping. It was truly breath taking. The T.V. in the kitchen was turned off. And there was no Baltimore Sun paper on the island today. There was only The New York Times and even sections of it were missing. Derrick opened the stainless steel fridge pouring himself a large glass of Tropicana orange juice. He sat at the kitchen island wondering where everyone was. Usually they would be having breakfast at the table and Dr. Jones would be checking his stocks in the Wall Street

Journal. Derrick turned on the T.V. and was immediately greeted by Nikki and her mom.

"Derrick turn the T.V. off please. I need to talk to you" said Nikki standing next to her mom who was trying desperately not to sob but couldn't restrained the flow of tears flowing down her cheeks.

"Are you ok Mrs. Jones?" he said with a concerned voice handing her a paper towel to wipe her eyes. They had already heard the news about Derrick moms grotesque murder and wanted to tell him before he found out from any media source. Nikki knew Derrick would go off like a time bomb. He and his mom shared a special bond and he was gonna explode like a bomb regardless the source of revelation about her treacherous death. His mom was killed in cold blood and he was determined to terminate the lives of all parties responsible; regardless of the circumstances. The following day Derrick surpassed his one hour run to two hour run. His martial arts skills were at their peak and his quest for revenge thrived deep within the core essence of his bone marrow. It was like the sweet revenge initiated by Fred Williamson, Jim Brown, and Jim Kelly in (Three The Hard Way.) Derrick however was going solo. And he was a one man army.

CHAPTER 38

It was now December 25th 2001, and the night of Q's Christmas party extravaganza at his elaborate 60 acre Greenspring estate. His annual Christmas/New Year's Eve party was well underway. All of his usual guest were arriving many of whom were already fucked up off of drugs and alcohol. You name it, Q had it. From cocaine to weed and heroin. The best that money could buy; all of the drugs supplied at his parties were free for those of his guest that cared to indulge. During the holidays Q would even do a few lines of coke himself. He'd stopped snorting on a regular bases. He learned early on from that mistake kicking a daily habit which almost caused him to fall off like so many dealers he knew that became their own best customer becoming major losers. It was ironic how many hustlers went from being major dealers to junkies losing everything; some even lost their minds. Derrick parked his new motor cycle on the side of the road outside of Q's estate. He'd purchased a Ninja motor cycle just a few weeks ago from the wife of a Naval lieutenant whose husband had been deployed overseas in Japan for the past 3 months. His overseas tour wouldn't be up for another 3 months and rumors of his infidelity proved to be true. He'd started dating this beautiful Geisha girl he'd met and fell madly in love with just two months into his tour.

His wife knew something was up. She could tell by his lack of words and enthusiasm about their relationship when he called home, which was once every other day. But soon became once a month. He finally told her he wanted out of the marriage. Out of spite she parked his Ninja motor cycle on the lawn and put a "FOR SALE" sign on it.

Derrick only paid $1,500.00 for a $7,000.00 bike. He had offered to pay her more.

He knew it was extremely underpriced and didn't want to get over on her for not knowing any better. But she was well aware of what she was doing and her motive wasn't money it was sweet revenge. And her husband was gonna be totally pissed when he came home on leave to find out his Ninja bike which was his pride and joy; SOLD.

Derrick was quite familiar with Q's estate. After the big toast would be the best time to take him out. It was now 11:45pm and 15 minutes til toast time. Derrick remained parked off the main road just a few yards down the road from Q's estate being sure not to arouse suspicion. By the time he scaled the 6ft. white privacy fence surrounding the estate it was 11:59pm Everyone raised their drinks in preparation to toast. Derrick posted himself outside the dining room window discretely watching Q's every move.

Derrick looked like a ferocious Lion pacing back and forth outside the window staring at Q like he was his prey and he couldn't wait to devour him. The angel of death was in the air.

Q would have a big toast every Christmas party at 12 mid-night, as if it were New Year's Eve. "5,4,3,2,1 Salute!" exclaimed Q as everyone lifted glasses of champagne. Q motioned to Big R who caught the signal excusing themselves from the rest of the party and went to his pool room located in the basement of his estate to snort a few lines of coke as they did every year. But little did they know this year they wouldn't be alone.

Derrick knew every sq. inch of Q's elaborate piece of land. And he knew exactly where they were going when they headed toward the back stair case. After all he should since he was once Q's top security guard and enforcer. Q walked over to his wall safe which was located behind a 24 X 30 portrait of himself and his late comrade Rodriquez from back in the day in Miami. Q removed about a gram of fish scale powdered cocaine from a zip-lock bag. The cocaine was so pure it sparkled as it hit the glass mirrored table. He exhaled slowly sitting on his black leather sofa in front of the mirror and began to form several perfect lines of the crystalized blow with a straight razor. Before he commenced to snort he looked over at the picture of he and Rodriquez once more. Although Q was held with the reverence of a king of valor to his drug kingpin affiliates, business associates, and soldiers he was a very lonely and depressed man. The only thing that had ever really brought him real joy was his beautiful daughter

Tina. Deep within Q's core self he trusted no one and little did he know he was about to feast lines of cocaine with his worst enemy whom he thought was a loyal comrade. The irony; most men of power were always deceived by those closest to them.

Every man regardless of his demeanor and level of authority and accomplishment had vulnerabilities and the Christmas holiday was Q's greatest moment of weakness.

Regardless of the fact he was a self-made street millionaire and cold blooded killer when necessary; he was still human and susceptible to human emotions. Even though many looked at him as a God due to his hard core and powerful exterior they failed to realize he too experienced moments of fear, loneliness, sadness and on occasion cried. Contrary to his hard core exterior he to needed love. And it was something about the Christmas and New Year holiday that always made him recollect the same feelings of loneliness and abandonment. He felt this pain since he was a child and it always surfaced from the inner child of his personality around the Christmas holiday. That was the main reason he always had plenty of people around him during the holiday season, in attempt to compensate for several years of lost love, affection, and family from his early youth. Q was forced to grow up fast and never experienced a real childhood being he was abandoned at the age of 6 years old. His mom had demons of her own battling a heroin addiction which eventually claimed her life.

As much as she loved her son she had no idea that her neglect would make him the victim of sexual abuse perpetrated by a male friend she shot dope with and she thought she could trust. A sick sexual predator that would fuck anything with an orifice. It was a cold winter night in Baltimore, Md. Q's original home town before moving to and growing up in LA. The bitter cold Baltimore air was chilling in December at around 24 degrees. He and his mom were moving from house to house and shelter to shelter seeking warmth. However, her primary objective was finding somewhere to shoot up and enjoy her dope. 6 year old Q tossed and turned trying his best to make himself comfortable in the run down dilapidated west Baltimore building he and his mom were put up in for the time being. It was the tenth place they'd stayed at that week, but this one he would never forget. While he laid in his innocence trying to sleep the dope fiend molester pressed his knee on Q's back pinning him down to a make shift bed made of blankets on the floor. "Get off me mister. Please let me go!" Q cried fighting for his manhood. But he was over powered and scared motionless by the dope fiend molester. Tears streamed down Q's tiny little face he cried and screamed from the agonizing pain he experienced from penetration from the sick pervert on top of him. "You like that boy?" "Was it good to you?" the molester exclaimed. "You tight just like your mama you little bitch, if you ever tell anybody about this I'm a kill you and her ass!!" "You hear me boy!" the sick molester yelled pressing his knee in Q's back once more."

Q never answered. He was in a state of shock. He had no idea what just happened to him but he knew it wasn't right or anything he would want to happen to him again. One thing he knew for sure was that he wanted to kill the sick bastard that had just violated him.

By the time Q was 8 years old he and his mom moved to LA seeking a change. She was entered into a drug program there that provided temporary custody of her son while she attempted to kick her drug habit. Upon release from the rehab she did great but eventually relapsed falling back into the same pattern and her dope fiend mentality soon followed. Nothing mattered more than her next fix. Out of desperation to get his mom to quit Q told her about the incident with the dope fiend molester back in Murdaland. She was devastated. She wanted to go back to Baltimore and kill that sick bastard. But, word on the street was the sick fucker had over dosed on some bad dope.

Q was disappointed when he heard of his death because he wanted the pleasure of killing the sick fuck himself. Q's mom felt so much guilt and pain for not being there to protect her son she began to self-destruct. Two weeks later she was found dead with a spike in in her arm. Her OD was intentional. As far as she was concerned she'd failed to protect her pride and joy from one of the worst things that could ever happen to a little boy. Her guilt and shame led her to become another statistic. Little did she know her son was strong and even though he knew what happened to him wasn't right he wasn't gonna allow that negative experience to define him and his manhood. From that point on he had serious trust issues and would often experience moments of loneness and depression.

CHAPTER 39

Over the years it was only four people Q allowed into his circle of trust. The pool hall owner Paul that took him in as a kid and taught him how to shoot pool at age ten. His late comrade and brother in-law Rodriquez from Bogota Colombia that taught him how to sell cocaine, his trusted comrade Big R. and Derrick his once loyal enforcer whom he'd grown to love as his own son that he felt betrayed him. That's why his quest for revenge against Derrick was so extreme and personal. The reason why Q ordered the removal of Derrick's mom's heart with a chain saw at the hands of some his most treacherous goons.

The opening of her chest with a chain saw and snatching her heart out was one of the most heinous crimes of the century. Yet Q felt no remorse. He felt vindicated. As far as he was concerned he was only taking back what he'd paid for from the mother of a selfish ungrateful bastard that betrayed his trust. Which was all an assassination of Derrick's character initiated by Big R because of his jealousy and greed. As far as he was concerned Derrick was a threat and he wanted him eliminated regardless of Q's code.

But little did he know his deception would be the cause of his own brutal death.

Derrick entered the basement door with no problem disabling the alarm before it could be activated. He stood face to face with his victims who were so fucked up off the cocaine they were snorting they thought they were seeing a ghost. Big R damn near shit himself. He immediately stepped two paces to the left away from Q in attempt to distance himself. He knew Derrick was out for blood because of what Q did to his mom.

The word of Derrick's moms brutal death was all over the news and he knew Derrick was there seeking revenge. The ass whipping his goons put on Derrick could never compare to what Q had done. At least that was

Big R's twisted reasoning. Q on the other hand was not intimidated. He felt insulted. "You dare show up here to my house after you stole from me you greedy son of a bitch, after all I did for you. I made you nigga.

I saved your mother's life. And the gratitude you show me in return was hitting my stash houses. I trusted you motherfucker. What was it? That bitch Nikki talked you into robbing me. It's always a bitch ain't it" "You can't trust dem whores" Big R. smirked making Q even that more infuriated. "Shut the fuck up R. she was your bitch nigga" Q said slamming his fist onto the pool table. "I told you she was a piece of work Derrick, but you fell for her anyway and let her talk you into taking my shit, you and that bitch are walking dead far as I'm concerned" Derrick had heard enough. "Shut the fuck up you simple ass motherfucker! It wasn't Nikki or me that betrayed you. That girl practically worshiped the ground you walked on Q. She had much respect for you man.

It was that fat fuck right there!!" Derrick exclaimed pointing his finger at Big R.

He set me up Q. think about it. Who else would know the best time to rob your stash houses. And if I robbed you I wouldn't need guns or a fuckin goon squad. I could take them motherfuckers out by my damn self. You know my pedigree"

Q stood looking dumb founded. There was a strong sense of truth emanating from Derrick. And even though he was still a lil fucked up from the coke he'd just been snorting what Derrick was saying made sense. He was so blinded by Big R's manipulation and Derrick and Nikki's absence he never really entertained the intricate details of what had truly transpired. Instead he assumed Big R was correct in naming Derrick as the culprit. Q looked Big R directly in the eyes and demanded the truth."

You set young blood up man?" "You mean to tell me it was you all this time" Big R was speechless. Beads of sweat formed his forehead and began dripping down his face like rain. "Motherfucker!!!" Q said taking a step back removing a Glock 9mm from the small of his back which was hid beneath his shirt. Even Derrick was shocked. This was something new. Because he never knew Q to carry a fire arm on him. Especially in his own home and at the big party. This was a time he usually had his guard down.

Evidently a lot had changed since Derrick last saw Q. He now trusted no one, at no time. Q was out of striking range so Derrick held his hands down to the side and was attempting to remove a throwing star from his waist band, but Q was all too familiar with his tactics. "Keep still nigga. You move again I'm blowin your fuckin head off. Q's Glock 9mm was pointed directly at Derricks head.

"Shoot dat nigga Q!" yelled Big R retrieving a 44. magnum from a holster beneath his suit jacket. "Shoot dat nigga or I will!!" Big R attempted to raise his 44. mag. In Derricks direction when he was caught by two nine millimeter slugs between the eyes. His body collapsed lifelessly to the ground like an animated cartoon character; it was surreal.

Derrick stared in dis belief. Little did he know the remaining moments of the next few minutes that unfolded would be up to him. Q was a man of honor and a man of his word.

He knew he'd made a terrible mistake in blaming Derrick for robbing his stash houses.

And most of all wrong for ordering a hit on his mom who died a horrible death.

Although Q was ruthless he still lived by a creed. A code that separated men from boys and Generals from soldiers. He knew Big R many years and he could tell he was lying.

Big R was never one to fold under pressure but his nervousness and inability to maintain eye contact with Q assured him he'd been betrayed. And the penalty was death. Now he must settle with Derrick. A man whom he'd loved like a son and trusted, then blamed for stealing from him. "I'm sorry young blood. Looks like I fucked up this time"

He said placing his Glock 9mm on the pool table maintaining eye contact with Derrick whose heart began to pump with adrenaline. The thought of throwing his razor sharp star between Q's eyes was a fraction of a second away from being manifested. "We can settle this like men Derrick" Q said moving to the center of the floor. "I know your gonna whip my ass but to shoot you would've been cowardly as far as I'm concerned because I was wrong" "We will settle this like men"

Derrick was confused. He knew Q had to know he was no match for him. And that Derrick was capable of killing him with his bare hands. But this is what made Q who his was. A true man of valor. Death before dis honor. Derrick respected Q's valor but that didn't change the fact he was about to whip his ass. "Fuck you!" yelled Derrick motioning forward throwing a solid kick to Q's abdomen sending him flying helplessly against the wall. Q's eyes stared forward as he attempted to regain his composure before being met with a flurry of kicks and punches to his head and body. Q never got a punch off. Derrick stepped to the side as Q's body fell to the floor. The next martial arts move would be an executing kill technique in which Derrick would leap into the air and come forcibly down with all his Ki and center of gravity crushing Q's sternum which was the part of the rib cage that protected the heart. This blow would crush Q's heart killing him instantly. Derrick was filled with rage and fury. He leaped four feet in the air with his knees drawn to his chest. He proceeded to land forcibly with his legs fully extended and feet together at an impeccable force.

The cracking sound of Q's rib cage echoed the room as Derricks feet smashed his heart and lungs like grapes in a vineyard.

The combination of Derrick's Ki power and execution of his lethal martial arts technique was deadly. Q's eyes bulged looking like they were about to pop out of his head. Blood and mucus spat out of his mouth as he gasped his last breath.

It was over.

Derrick returned to Nikki's parents estate and he and Nikki packed their things and moved South. A little town not far from where Reds and Tonya had moved too after the massacre at the club Dynasty.

CHAPTER 40

It was ironic how this little Virginia town was becoming a means of refuge for those seeking a new beginning on life. Things weren't going to great at the moment between Reds and Tonya. Seven years had passed. The economical climate of society was headed toward a major change. Over the next couple years several businesses would collapse, jobs would be lost, home owners would go into foreclosure, and America would have its very first black president named, Barack Obama. He would inherit an economic nightmare created by several administrations prior to his taking office that left his administration with the responsibility of cleaning up the mess.

The year was now 2012 and the slogan sweeping society was Corporate Greed.

A slogan which opened a Pandora's box to societies dissatisfaction with Americas prosperity which seemed to favor those with money and power. The top 1% of Americas elite that not only pulled the strings but also pushed the buttons. The paradox of Hustlers Greed and Corporate Greed were synonymous. Survive by; "Any means necessary" Which was the creed that severed as motivation on every echelon; From Street Hustler$ with millions of dollars stashed in cash; To Corporate Executive$ with million dollar parachutes guaranteed by Corporate America. The American dream had become the American nightmare and for Reds it was no exception. After the massacre at The Club Dynasty and the murder of his comrade Rockman he swore he was done with the drug game. However after foreclosure on several properties he owned and the collapse of his production company he was left with no alternative than to go back to what he knew best in times of survival. The drug game. Something he'd promised Tonya he was done with. But, Reds was a true hustler, born and breed from a creed which came from a fabric of cloth that only the realest of the real manifested. You could take a hustler out the game, but you couldn't take the game out the hustler. If there was a way to make money he'd find it. Especially when he was hungry.

After his first foreclosure notice Reds began rebuilding his own Lil drug organization.

Making fast money was never a stranger to him. Reds partnered with a few hustlers in Va. selling weed, which was a means of steady income. He would buy weight wholesale and sell to local hustlers at retail prices making at least an extra $1,500.00 to $2,000.00 a week; which was nothing compared to the $1,500.00 to $2,000.00 a day he would make in the drug game selling cocaine. Initially Reds would just make his drug runs to PA, to meet his seller on the weekends to pick up his weed. There were many exotic brands of weed out and at the moment (Nitro diesel) was the killer shit. Reds was buying it by the pound spending $4,000.00 to $5000.00 a pop, but quickly doubled and tripled his money when he sold it back on the streets to local dealers in VA. by the ounce.

It seems weed sales were almost as profitable as cocaine, except for the eighties when Crack was booming. Wasn't no money like crack rock money. If you set up shop right and had a good run with a good team you could make a quick million in no time. Tonya and Reds relationship became more and more distant. She knew he was back in the drug game and wanted no parts of it. After the massacre at the club Dynasty she was terrified and wanted no more parts of that lifestyle.

She thought the life she and Reds began in Virginia with their son and daughter was a new beginning. She'd been a hustler's girl and wanted no more parts of that life. With the launch of her modeling agency and his production company she felt they would be financially straight. But the production company had bottomed out. He'd lost a lot of money promoting various artist that never jumped off big in the music industry, especially after 911 and the stock market crash that led to the great recession. So Reds soon returned to what he knew best; hustling, even though Tonya had made enough monies from her modeling agency to hold them over. Reds refused to be carried. He was his own man. And shit was really about to hit the fan now that Kilo was back on the streets. Reds and some of his new crew was in his club basement shooting pool smoking weed when he first heard of Kilo's release. Reds had always sworn revenge on Kilo after the massacre at the Dynasty and he was determined to kill that nigga for killing his comrade Rockman and destroying their criminal empire. Everyone always wondered what happened to Reds and Tonya. A lot of people thought they were killed in the blazing inferno at the Club Dynasty. And that's the way Reds wanted it. He wanted them to be presumed dead so he and Tonya could have a new beginning but Reds was a street nigga at heart and was determined to someday seek out his revenge on Kilo. He lived by the street code and would die by it if he had too.

CHAPTER 41

Reds had packed a bag which concealed his Glock 9mm and a few other personal items such as deodorant and his tooth brush. In his other hand he carried a big duffle bag, which tilted his body weight slightly to right side. "I gotta bounce for a few days babe" he said as he came down the stairs kissing her on the forehead sitting the heavy duffle bag on the floor. "Bounce, where to Reds? I'm sick of this outta town shit. I have enough money to carry us. You know you don't have to do that shit no more" Tonya smirked at Reds with a look of distain as she turned to walk away. "Hold up babe" he said grabbing her gently by the arm. "It' s not about the money. I got loot" Tonya stopped and looked at Reds with a look of bewilderment; a look that could tame the hardest street nigga. Her beautiful brown eyes and exotic features were stunning. And her body was killa. Her long lean legs were endless in the pair of Baby Phat shorts she flaunted which complimented her perfectly round yellow ass. If you didn't know Tonya was African American and Indian you would think she was Puerto Rican or Dominican. She was a fuckin stunner. And the look she gave Reds made him second guess just what the fuck was he thinking. Why in the hell was he about to risk not ever seeing his beautiful woman again in a quest of revenge for his comrades that were killed almost nine years ago. Needless to say he was taking a chance of not ever seeing his son and daughter again who were his pride and joy.

Reds sat the duffle bag of money on the floor next to Tonya which contained about $180,000.00 in rubber band stacks of hundreds, fifty's, twenties, and ones. "Here babe, put this up for emergency. I'm a be gone a few weeks" Tonya and Reds also had platinum colored Audi's. A 2012 Q7 Quattro and A8 which Reds usually drove. Both paid in full; He was leaving the A8 with her. He decided to take a rental as he usually did when going out of town. Reds handed her the keys to the Audi A8 kissing her gently on the lips. Tonya looked at Reds with a look of total disappointment. "Fuck you mean you leaven Reds. You don't have to keep doin this shit. We're ok!" Tonya had made almost a quarter million dollars from her modeling agency over the past year. And was the kinda chick that would hold her man down. But Reds was a go-getta and the kinda hustler that was use to making his own loot. But this trip wasn't about money, it was about revenge.

"There some things I gotta take care of sweetie. I'll be back as soon as possible" Tonya rolled her eyes at Reds. "Yeah ok Michael. You go ahead. Do what you gotta do. I'm sick of this shit. I thought we were movin forward and here your dumb ass go running back to the past" Reds knew she was really upset because she called him by his government name; Michael. "Fuck you talkin bout Tonya?" Reds had no idea Tonya knew about Kilo being released from prison. However his release was televised nationwide. "You know what the fuck I'm talkin bout Reds, I'm not stupid. You goin back to Baltimore to kill Kilo for killing Rockman and burning down yall club.

And you gonna be dead right along with them. You know Kilo connected. That nigga got more protection than the Pope.

Your dumb ass won't get close to him" at this point Reds was getting pissed. "Shut the fuck up man, you don't know what the hell you talkin bout. I got this. That nigga good as dead by the time I see him" "Yeah well stand in line Michael, because you not the only one that want that nigga dead if so he would've been dead a long time ago. He's too smart and too protected" now Reds was really getting angry. "Fuck outta here so what you saying that nigga smarter than me." Tonya walked over to Reds placing her head on his shoulder. "No baby, I know you're smart. I'm just saying Kilo is relentless and a cold blooded killer. You're not. You're a hustler baby and a damn good one, but you're not a killer" Reds left it at that. He had killed before in a few drug deals that had gone bad, but at this point in his life it was unnecessary to disclosed that information to Tonya. What difference would it make and that made him think. He would be taking a chance of losing everything if he sought revenge on Kilo. At this point in his life it wasn't just about him anymore he had a son and daughter that worshiped the ground he walked on and a woman that loved him with all her heart and soul. He had already been given a second chance to start over and at what point would he learn. Most of his comrades were either dead or incarcerated for life. Reds looked Tonya in her beautiful brown eyes and kissed her gently on her forehead. Tears of joy began to stream down her cheeks and the most beautiful smile formed her face. Damn Reds thought to himself. This beautiful woman standing before me may have just saved my life; needless to say his freedom. He felt like the most loved and blessed man on the face of the earth. Only a fool would mess that up.

CHAPTER 42

The following week Reds booked a vacation get away for he and Tonya. The destination was somewhere remote and exotic. It's ironic because just a few months prior to this whole ordeal Reds and Tonya had planned a family vacation to Hawaii. But after the events that had unfolded over the past few weeks they felt a need to get away sooner.

Somewhere beautiful, exotic and far away from everything. Their destination, The Florida Keys. A one week stay in Key West for just the two of them. Life was always full of surprises and the next seven days were no exception. The Florida Keys was becoming quite popular and would be quite memorable. How ironic the same place Reds and Tonya sought to escape memories from their past and start a new beginning would possibly bring them face to face with their most hated adversary, Kilo . . . .

Kilo and Tina were still on the island of Key West attempting to put their lives back together after his incarceration and near escape from death by lethal injection. For the first time in life he felt a desire to do something different then run the criminal empire he headed with the help of his cousin KG for the past fifteen years. He too had lost many comrades to the drug game. Including his good childhood friend Tyrone. And it wasn't a day that passed Kilo didn't feel responsible for the death of Tyrone's lil brother Jessie who aided him in the massacre at the club Dynasty. Kilo was now experiencing his moment of truth. For so long his life had been a never ending cycle of death, death and, more death . . . .

At this point in Kilo's life he wanted to embrace life. Kilo had so much money, power, and respect he could afford any luxury he so desired. The one thing he could never buy was his way out of the drug game. He was in too deep. His only way out was death.

All he wanted at this point in his life was for the moments he and Tina shared together on their little island villa to last forever. But unfortunately nothing lasted for ever; good or bad in this lifetime . . . .

Chapter 43

It was just a little after midnight. Kilo and Tina were at the bar having drinks. The mood and atmosphere for the evening was quite delightful. Soon all hell was about to break loose. The 80 degree temperature was complimented by a cool tropical island breeze and beautiful full moon lite sky which set the mood for a very romantic night.

Reds and Tonya had just finished checking into a very eloquent island resort. They changed quickly into more suitable island attire. He wore a pair of tan khakis with a blue Rocawear shirt and blue and white Jordan's. Tonya wore a beautiful blue Yves Saint Laurent skirt showing off her beautiful long legs and a pair of lo cut Jimmy Choo sandals which demanded the attention of every woman that caught their eye. It was the first thing Tina noticed as Reds and Tonya approached the bar.

Tonya was intrigued by Tina's beautiful Jimmy Choo hand bag which complimented her sandals perfectly. Both women were actually very intrigued by each other's beauty, styles, and class which were quite similar, but nonchalant in displaying their observations. Which was quite the opposite for Kilo and Reds who gave each other a look of death as soon as their eyes connected. Reds and Tonya seated themselves at the crowded bar a few seats way from Kilo and Tina. "What's your pleasure?" asked the bar tender politely. "Death!" answered Reds starring at Kilo. The bar tender was totally bewildered and so was Tonya until she saw Reds and Kilo locked in an evil eyed stare with each other. Her hand began to tremble as she placed it on Reds forearm.

"OMG!!!" she thought to herself. Reds gonna kill him. At that moment Kilo and Reds both stood to their feet in preparation to fight to the death. "Fuck you staring at Reds?"

"You bitch!!!!" yelled Reds as he lunged at Kilo with a punch that would've knocked out a mule if he'd connected. Kilo evaded the punch with a side step just inches from his chin. They were now both standing in the middle of the bar with a floor full of spectators looking on eagerly as if two gladiators were about to battle to their deaths. Tonya and Tina both immediately took to their men's side. Tina slid her hand inside her Jimmy choo hand bag grasping the handle of a seven inch switch blade knife which she was prepared to pull out cutting anyone that crossed her path.

The next punch thrown by Reds was a right hook connecting with the left side of Kilo's jaw sending him falling into the bar. At that moment the sound of Tina's switch blade knife opening and the swish of the blade missing Reds face by inches had everyone on the edge of their seats starring in awe. Tonya leaped on Tina grabbing her knife wielding hand like a snake charmer apprehending a snake. Tonya and Tina wrestled with the knife until they were both on the ground. At that moment island security intervened separating the two couples taking all of them to a small room. This wasn't the first time a few island locals had a bit too much to drink and quarreled and it definitely wouldn't be the last. However little did island authorities know they had two arch rivals in their presence with a history of violence that went back many years. Kilo and Reds remained cool while in the custody of island authorities knowing any further display of violence would possibly get them both barred off the island or even arrested. They both had lengthy crime records and it was no need to rock the boat. Was this fate or just bad timing? Over a hundred islands make up the Keys all joined together by a 126 miles of road and it was ironic Kilo and Reds would end up on the same island, at the same fucking time, at the same night life spot. After a lengthy lecture by island officials, Kilo and Tina, along with Reds and Tonya agreed to end their beef. They exited the back office jovial laughing and joking as if they were longtime friends. But at this point they had to work together.

"Yo son, you gotta a mean right hook" laughed Kilo holding his jaw. "I thought I got hit by Floyd Mayweather !" It was funny, even though Kilo was born in New York and raised in Baltimore city he always maintained his New York accent. "Ahh Baby!" Tina said. Kissing Kilo's face rolling her eyes at Red's for hurting her Boo as they all walked back towards the bar. "Excuse me." said Kilo motioning towards one of the bar maids.

"Is there any way possible my friends and I could get that spot right there?" at that moment Kilo grasped the tender right hand of the bar maid with a gentle caress placing a folded hundred dollar bill in the center of her palm. "Oh yes sir, no problem blushed the bar maid I believe that booths all yours" she was still smiling. Tina glanced the pretty young bar maid up and down giving her a look of. "OK bitch get our table and keep it moving!" Kilo was no stranger to accommodative hospitality. Needless to say he had class, charm, swag and plenty of loot. On any given night with a wealthy patron like Kilo a bar maid could make almost a grand for just keeping the ice cold on a bottle of champagne. And tonight was no exception. Kilo ordered a two bottles of Ace a Spades at $600.00 a bottle. He Tina, Reds, and Tonya sat at their private booth getting totally fucked up. And the night was still young . . . . After a few hours on the dance floor acting total fools and enjoying themselves as if it were their last days on this earth. Kilo and Reds finally had their moment of truth. The fact they were arch enemies who would've once given their right leg to see the other dead, at this moment was irrelevant.

Kilo and Reds were two stand up guys who once shared a common hatred toward one another driven by a rivalry created by Rockman and his greed. They were now at a crossroad of fate and the more they drank, laughed, and had fun, the more they became cool. "Here's a toast to the good times, bad times, and moments of truth" said Kilo raising his glass as Reds, Tina, and Tonya joined in. After the toast Tina and Tonya became engaged in conversation on all of the latest fashions, trends, and hateration they often experienced from jealous bitches that hated them because they were well kept and pampered with their every heart's desire by men. Kilo and Reds on the other hand were on some real G shit; Two O.G's who had seen and done it all in terms of the drug game over the years, they had made a lot of money, had a lot of fun, and witnessed a lot of death. Some with their own hands. "You know Reds you aight homie. I always had much respect and admiration for you. You a standup guy. But your man Rockman was bad news. He was shittin on everybody man. That night after we hit the club I heard you picked up Tonya and balled out of town. If it got that hot for me I would've done the same thing G. Some of my comrades had followed you from your condo in Owings mills when you picked up her in your Lexus coupe and rolled out. They wanted to make a move on you but I said, NO!

That's because I never had a beef with you man and had much respect for you as a hustler; you wasn't a grimy nigga. And I never considered you an enemy.

It was many days man I'd wish you were down with me and my team. Real niggas that's true to the game are rare these days. Everyman is out for his self.

Cats be doin more bitchin and snitchin then pitchin and hittin. Feel me?"

Reds laughed glancing over at Tonya who appeared to be having the time of her life. He hadn't seen her have that much fun in years. "I feel you my nigga, ha, ha . . . I feel you" said Reds taking another sip of Aces of Spades." "This some smooth shit right here too homie." smiled Reds. "I'm usually a Henny man" "Oh yeah I fucks wit da Henny too; XO cognac is smooth" responded Kilo. "Good shit!" it was a good night.

And ironic how two hustlers who were just about to kill each other were now chillin like Goodfellas. At that moment the owner of the club sent over two Cuban cigars to Kilo and Reds; Who showed much appreciation as they lit up. They figured the club owner was happy they'd settled their differences and didn't shoot up his joint. The fresh rolled Cuban cigars went perfect with their Ace Of Spades. After a few more days of exotic sun rays and fun nights on the beautiful Key West island of paradise. Reds and Tonya where headed back to Baltimore on the private jet with Kilo and Tina. The illustrious million dollar luxury jet flew through the beautiful picture perfect, Florida Keys blue sky with great precision and tranquility.

Kilo, Tina, Reds, and Tonya toasted with glasses of raspberry Ciroc 500 feet above sea level. Kilo lead the toast. "Here's to continued life, health, wealth, and good fortune. "Sky's the limit!" "Sky's the limit!!!" responded Reds, Tonya, and Tina. "CLING!!"

CHAPTER 44

The private jets ETA to BWI/Thurgood Marshall airport was two and a half hours.

Facebook and Twitter was buzzing with a spectacular party at Baltimore's Eden Lounge; tonight's event sponsored by The CirocBoy crew for everyone looking to have fun and socialize with good quality people. Konan and the beautiful Erica Kane were echoing the sound waves on 92Q jams with a DJ K-Swift memorial tribute playing some of Baltimore's best club jams. Baltimore was known as the Murdaland, but it was truly a city of remarkable talent and ambition. A city like many others where poverty and prosperity were only a zip code away; like New York and L.A. where dreams can come true with hard work and perseverance. A city of many choices, professional occupations, and much opportunity: Nevertheless, Kilo and Reds would always be hustler's. It was ironic after so many years of planning and preparation how he would kill Kilo if ever in his presence how Reds would become one of his most trusted comrades in an occupation where few drug dealers have longevity even with loyalty and creed, because you can never underestimate a certified hustler's greed . . . .

The End

BY: Martin L. Stockton